"A celebration of faith, family, and the human spirit, *The Golfer's Carol* is a page-turning story of love and second chances that is sure to become a classic. The four inspiring lessons will stay with readers long after the last page is turned."
—Winston Groom, author of *Forrest Gump*

"At some point in our lives, most golfers like to imagine playing a round of golf with our sporting heroes, a heavenly foursome comprised of the greats of the game and maybe a missing loved one. In his wee gem of a book, *The Golfer's Carol*, Robert Bailey creates both a hymn to the heroes of golf and a moving fable about what is most important—and enduring—to learn from the game. The moral rings clear: It's never too late to have a Wonderful Life. George Bailey couldn't have told the story any better!"
—James Dodson, author of *Ben Hogan: An American Life*

"A fun, fast read, this novel kind of sneaks its wisdom up on you. I thought it splendid."
—Homer Hickam, author *Rocket Boys* and
Carrying Albert Home

"Inspiring . . . Sharp in its dialogue, real with its relationships, and fascinating in details of the game, *The Golfer's Carol* is that rarest of books—one you will read and keep for yourself, while purchasing multiple copies for friends."
—Andy Andrews, author of *The Noticer* and *The Traveler's Gift*

THE
GOLFER'S
CAROL

Robert Bailey

G. P. PUTNAM'S SONS
New York

PUTNAM
— EST. 1838 —
G. P. Putnam's Sons
Publishers Since 1838
An imprint of Penguin Random House LLC
penguinrandomhouse.com

The Library of Congress has catalogued
the G. P. Putnam's Sons hardcover edition as follows:

Names: Bailey, Robert, author.
Title: The golfer's carol / Robert Bailey.
Description: New York: G. P. Putnam's Sons, 2020.
Identifiers: LCCN 2020018129 | ISBN 9780593190500 (hardcover) |
ISBN 9780593190517 (ebook)
Subjects: GSAFD: Mystery fiction.
Classification: LCC PS3602.A5495 G65 2020 | DDC 813/.6—dc23
LC record available at https://lccn.loc.gov/2020018129
p.   cm.

First G. P. Putnam's Sons hardcover edition / November 2020
First G. P. Putnam's Sons trade paperback edition / October 2022
G. P. Putnam's Sons trade paperback edition ISBN: 9780593190524

Printed in the United States of America
1st Printing

Book design by Ashley Tucker

For my children: Jimmy, Bobby, and Allie

PRACTICE TEE

1

WEDNESDAY, APRIL 9, 1986. 6:30 A.M.

"There comes a point in every man's life when he realizes that he's not going to be Joe Namath." Sixteen years ago, that was my father's way of telling me that my dreams of being a professional golfer had no chance of coming true.

What does a famous football player have to do with the game of golf? Well, nothing, when you look at it that way. But in the spring of 1970, pretty much every red-blooded male in the state of Alabama dreamed of being Joe Willie Namath, the strong-armed, good-looking quarterback of the New York Jets, who before turning pro and becoming "Broadway Joe" had led the Alabama Crimson Tide football team to two national championships.

I understood exactly what my dad was telling me, but he went ahead and broke it down just in case.

"What I'm trying to say, son, is that not everybody can be the star of the football team. Or a movie star. Or . . . even a golfer on the PGA Tour. God didn't bless us all with that type of talent. But he gives us other skills, Randy." He had looked at his hands then, and so had I. For forty years, my father, Robert Clark, had been a bricklayer. He had helped build houses all over north Alabama. His hands were like two blocks of concrete. They were the tools of his trade.

"God has given you talents too, son." He had paused then, and again looked at his heavily callused hands. "He's also given you responsibilities."

Pulling myself from my reverie, I stood and felt the wind coming off the water hit my face. The Tennessee River Bridge, at its highest, is a good hundred feet from the surface of the water. If a person were to dive in headfirst, he would die in an instant. His body would wash up on the shore or be dug out by a boat dragging the river, but the person's spirit would be gone quicker than the ripples.

My spirit died in 1970. I was twenty-four years old. My golf game had sent me to the University of Alabama on a scholarship, and I had been good enough to make All-SEC. I had played the mini tours for a year and felt like I was close to breaking through. Just a few more putts going in. One less penalty shot. Keeping my mind focused. I was so close.

Then Mary Alice got pregnant, my game went to pot, and my dad told me that I couldn't be Joe Namath.

And life still had one more sucker punch left to throw.

TODAY IS MY FORTIETH BIRTHDAY, SO IT'LL BE SLIGHTLY DIF-ferent than every other day this week. I'll still go into the office. I'll still work nine hours and attempt to bill every second to an insurance company that is paying me to represent its insured in a car-wreck case. I'll still have a coffee break around ten thirty, and I'm sure I'll shoot the bull with Steve Ledyard. Steve's a big Auburn fan, so we'll probably rehash Alabama's victory over the Tigers in the prior year's Iron Bowl again and debate for the hundredth time whether Bo Jackson should play baseball or football. But around two thirty, the people in our department will gather in the small firm kitchen while my secretary, Debbie Seal, cuts the cake she bought at Kroger on the way to work. It'll taste okay, and they will all make jokes about the big 4-0. And then, at about the seven- or eight-minute mark, everyone will return to their jobs.

At around six fifteen, I'll walk to the elevator with my briefcase. Then I'll go home and there will be more cake, this time Mary Alice's homemade German chocolate, my favorite. Before we eat cake, we'll head down to Boots' Steakhouse. Our sixteen-year-old daughter, Davis, and I will split the prime rib and baked potato, while Mary Alice will have a few bites off our plate and stick to the salad. Then we'll come home. I'll blow out the candles. There will be exactly forty of them. Mary Alice is a details person, always has been. Then I'll eat a slice of cake, maybe even two. I'll brag on how good it tastes, because it will taste good. My wife is the best cook I've ever met. I'll help her with the dishes afterward and then we'll probably watch TV while Davis does her homework. After the ten o'clock news, we'll go to bed. We won't make love. We haven't in years.

THE NEXT DAY, MY WIFE WILL EXPECT ME TO WAKE UP AT six a.m., make a pot of coffee, read the newspaper, and give her a kiss on the cheek before heading to the office. She'll expect me to be home for dinner. That's been our life together for as long as we both can remember.

But tomorrow, Mary Alice and everyone else is in for a surprise. Tomorrow, I plan to wake an hour early and slip out of the house without a sound.

I'll drive to the bridge and stand exactly where I'm standing now. I'll wear my golf clothes. Collared shirt with a sweater over it, khaki slacks, and my FootJoy spikes. I won't say a prayer, because, though I used to go to church on Sundays and even served as an usher for years, I don't believe in God anymore. No, instead I'll repeat the words of my father, Robert Clark, on an early spring day in 1970.

There comes a point in every man's life when he realizes that he's not going to be Joe Namath.

And then, as the sun begins to rise over the Tennessee River, I'll jump.

2

YOU MIGHT SAY THAT MY BIRTHDAY DIDN'T PAN OUT THE WAY I thought it would. And that would be an understatement. Things got weird long before I saw the ghost of Darby Hays, but let's take them in the order in which they happened.

I left the Tennessee River Bridge at six forty a.m. and was at my office in downtown Huntsville by seven. I spent the morning preparing for and conducting a car-wreck plaintiff's deposition. When it finished sooner than I expected, I reviewed my life insurance policy one last time.

At eleven forty-five a.m., I decided to go out for lunch. I had made it halfway down the hallway when Debbie called after me. "Randy!"

I looked over my shoulder, and Debbie was leaning out of her cubicle. She had stretched the phone line as far as it would go, and she was holding the receiver out. "It's Mary Alice. She says it's important."

My stomach tightened as I registered the look of worry on my assistant's face. I tried not to speculate, but my first thought was that something had happened to Davis. My second was for my mother. Since Dad's death two years ago, Mom had kept busy with her friends and seemed to be in good health. But she was in her seventies, and life can change on a dime.

Shaking off the thoughts, I strode back to my office and picked up the phone, steeling myself for the worst.

"Is Davis okay?" I asked, forgoing any pleasantries.

"Randy, have you heard about Darby?"

I blinked, as relief flooded through me that my daughter and mother were okay. *Darby?* My friend's heavyset gait, bushy salt-and-pepper beard, and piercing blue eyes immediately came to mind. "No, what is it?"

"He was in a car accident last night in Birmingham." She paused, and I could tell she was trying hard not to cry. "He's dead, Randy. I'm so sorry."

I lowered myself to my chair and stared through the yellow notepad on the desk. All I could see was my last memory of Darby. Standing on the tee box of the eighteenth hole at Shoal Creek, his home course, telling me that the PGA Champion-ship was coming back to Shoal in five years. Then he had hit his patented draw that started down the right side of the fairway and curved into the middle, coming to rest approximately 285 yards from the tee. He had the smoothest golf swing I've ever seen. "That'll do, Randolph!" Darby had yelled. I had followed with a good but not great tee shot that had come to rest on the right side of the fairway a good twenty yards behind Darby. Length off the tee was one of the strengths of Darby's game. It was one of the main reasons my friend and former teammate on the University of Alabama golf team had played nineteen years on the PGA Tour.

He's dead, I thought.

"Randy, are you there?"

"Yeah," I said, trying and failing to bring myself back to the present. When I had met him my freshman year, Darby was a senior and one of the finest college golfers in the country. The coach asked Darby to room with me on the road, and I initially wasn't sure what to make of my supposed mentor, who, from the first moment I was introduced to him, took to calling me "Randolph," when my real name was Randall and the only nickname I had ever had was Randy. But, like everyone else on the team, I eventually grew to idolize Darby's quick wit, laid-back manner, and unbelievable game. He was the only player I'd ever known who could stay out all night partying and still show up on the first tee and shoot under par. Darby let me tag along during many of his adventures, on and off the course, and we became good friends. After school, we remained close as his golf career took off and mine fizzled out. *He was my best friend*, I thought.

And now he's gone . . .

"Randy?" Mary Alice asked again, her voice an octave higher. "Are you okay?"

"Yeah," I lied. "I just . . . can't believe it. How did you find out?"

"Charlotte called. She said she was going to call you herself but didn't think she could get through it."

"How did it happen?"

"Darby had played eighteen holes at Shoal Creek, drank a couple gin and tonics, and left around seven. She doesn't know what he did after that, but the police found a half-drunk fifth of Bombay in the floorboard of the Jaguar."

I paused, remembering how much Darby loved his white Jaguar. *Randolph, this is the finest automobile made in the world*, he had said, the first time he'd taken me for a spin in his pride and joy. I felt tears forming in the corners of my eyes.

"How did Charlotte sound?"

"She was okay. I think she's madder at him right now than sad."

"Does she need anything? Should we—"

"No, she said the funeral would be Friday. Nothing fancy. Just a small service. Charlotte said that Darby would be livid if she scheduled his funeral to conflict with Masters coverage on the weekend."

I smiled and wiped the tears off my cheek. "That sounds like Darb."

For several seconds, silence filled the line. "Are you sure you're okay?" Mary Alice asked, her voice tentative. "Do you want to take the rest of the day off?"

I stood from my chair. "No . . . I can't. Debbie and some of the folks in our department have a cake for me and—"

"Your birthday," Mary Alice interrupted, sniffling. "I can't believe this would happen on your birthday. Randy, I'm so sorry."

Me too, I thought. "I'll see you tonight, hon. I'll be okay."

"If you don't feel like going out, I can make something here."

"Okay, we'll play it by ear," I said. "I need to go."

"Randy?"

"Yeah, hon."

"I love you."

I closed my eyes, thinking not of Darby Hays but of the hard surface and dirty water of the Tennessee River. "Love you too," I managed, before hanging up the phone.

3

I HAD ORIGINALLY PLANNED TO WALK TO GORIN'S, A SAND-wich and ice cream shop downtown, for lunch. I had wanted my last lunch on earth to be at one of my favorite places, and Gorin's had the best chicken fingers I'd ever tasted.

Instead, without much conscious thought, as if my mind had turned on autopilot after learning about Darby, I ended up driving to the Twickenham Country Club. Though my law firm provided few fringe benefits to associates, the partners had offered me, as the firm's only accomplished golfer, a corporate membership to the club. In return for this perk, which netted me ten rounds a year and access to the course and practice facilities for my children, I was expected to entertain clients and hustle new business.

Since our money troubles had begun three years ago, the only golf I allowed myself to enjoy other than obligatory outings with current or prospective clients was the few hours I was able to spend out here with Davis in the early evenings after work. Watching my beautiful, spunky daughter hit balls until her face and neck were covered with sweat and her brown hair was matted to the side of her head was about the only thing that gave me peace anymore.

Today, however, given the news I had just received and what I was planning to do tomorrow, I decided to go rogue. I went to the nineteenth-hole lounge and, in an ode to my dead friend, ordered a gin and tonic.

"Taking the day off, Mr. Clark?"

I turned to see Cary Harvella, the club's young assistant professional, who smiled and added, "Don't see you out here much anymore."

I nodded and took a sip of gin. "I know, but today . . ." My mind flashed images of Darby Hays wearing a white golf shirt and green slacks and striding down the thirteenth hole at Augusta ten years ago. Darby had gotten me a badge for Saturday's round that year, and I had followed him every hole. On thirteen, he'd strolled over to me, whistling as he was prone to do, and said, "Randolph, if I'm going to make any noise in this tournament, I need an eagle. Get your camera ready." He had then walked up to his ball, taken two drags off the cigarette he'd been puffing on, and launched a three wood right at the flag. The ball had landed on the front of the green, barely clearing Rae's Creek and coming to rest five feet from the pin. Darby had turned to me and taken a bow. It was the greatest golf shot I'd ever seen.

"Mr. Clark?" Cary's voice sounded like it was coming from a mile away, but, seeing his eyes crease with concern, I remembered myself.

"Today's my birthday, Cary. I figured I could squeeze in eighteen holes."

"Sounds good. I think the Big Team is going out at one o'clock. You might try to get in on that."

"Thanks for the tip," I said, draining the rest of the glass.

Cary looked at the empty cup and then at me. "You okay, Mr. Clark?"

"Fine. Just rewarding myself for making it to forty." I gestured at the bartender for a refill and smiled up at Cary. "Don't worry about me, son."

I took another long sip of gin from my refilled glass.

"Hey, Clark," a raspy voice yelled from over my shoulder.

"Yeah," I said, taking another sip and not turning around.

"The whole team's not here, but we got seven. We need another A player for one o'clock. You in or just drinking?"

"Who would be the players in my foursome?" I asked, making eye contact with Moq through the glass mirror above the bar.

"Simpson, Vowell, and Boone."

"And yours?"

"Coach, Finger, and Mule."

I smiled. Generally speaking, on the rare occasions when I played Big Team, I tried to avoid playing against the all-nickname group. It was bad for the bank account.

"You in or not, Clark?"

I drained the rest of the gin in one long sip and whirled around on the stool. I wondered why I hadn't thought of this before. My last afternoon in this godforsaken world ought to be spent on the golf course. I felt a twinge of regret about missing the office party that Debbie was throwing for me, but she would understand.

Thanks, Darb, I thought. Then, hopping off the stool, I pierced Moq with a glare. "So, what's the bet?"

4

I HAD NEVER PAID MUCH ATTENTION TO THE GAMBLING MI-
nutiae that made up the typical Big Team match. Simply put, it
was a birdie game. One foursome played another and the group
that made the most birdies won. Each group was made up of
an A, B, C, and D player, and the designations were based on
the golfer's USGA handicap. If a player didn't have an estab-
lished handicap, then he normally wasn't allowed in the match.
Sandbaggers—players who said their handicap was higher than
it actually was—were, at least in the eyes of the Twickenham
Country Club Big Team, the lowest scum on the face of the
earth.

I had a zero handicap, which meant I was a scratch golfer.
Unfortunately, my game was steadier than some of the other A
players, meaning I normally shot a good score with a lot of pars,
but I didn't make enough birdies to ever win much money. Perhaps it was the gin in my system or the fact that I had nothing to
lose since I planned to jump off the Tennessee River Bridge in
about eighteen hours, but I could do no wrong over the first nine

holes of play. Abandoning my typical conservative brand of play, I went for every pin and hit driver off every tee box of the tight, tree-lined course. I birdied the first six holes and drained a twenty-five-foot snake of a putt on nine for a twenty-nine.

After about the fifth hole, even my own teammates stopped talking to me. I usually made conversation with the other players in my group, but today I had hardly acknowledged them. Bland Simpson was our B player, and he had actually birdied two of the holes that I hadn't. Simpson was a developer who had a mean streak. When a new player had tried to break into the Big Team a few years back and had failed to bring enough money to cover what he owed, Simpson had clubbed the poor sap in his right kneecap with a seven iron. Suffice it to say, the guy never came back. The incident had gained Simpson a warning from the club brass that he'd be kicked out if anything like that happened again. But among the other men in the group, he became a legend.

"Course record is sixty-three," Simpson whispered as I downed another gin and tonic in the nineteenth hole at the turn.

I peered at him while I threw back the gin. "You're wrong," I said. "The course record is fifty-seven."

Simpson scratched his head and glared at me. "I've been a member here for fifteen years." He paused. "You calling me a liar, Clark?" He leaned closer and I could smell Miller Lite on his breath. Simpson typically drank a twelve-pack of beer during each round.

"No, I'm not. The recorded course record is sixty-three." I paused and drank the rest of my glass. "All I'm saying is that I watched someone shoot fifty-seven on this goat track five years ago. He didn't tell the club because he would never take a member's record."

Simpson smirked. "And who is this Good Samaritan?"

"A dead man," I said, winking at Bland and pushing off the stool.

MY GAME LOST SOME STEAM ON THE BACK NINE. ON ELEVEN, A short par five that was one of the easiest holes on the course, I went for the green in two and hooked my ball into the greenside pond. I took a bogey, and Simpson wasn't able to bail us out, only making par. The alcohol in my system had begun to slow my senses, and I started spraying tee shots left and right. Fortunately, the booze had loosened my nerves on the greens, and the putts were still falling. Despite my erratic ballstriking, I managed to scrounge up birdies on thirteen, fifteen, and sixteen.

As daylight began to fade, my emotions started to spill over. I kept envisioning Davis when she was eight years old, wearing a collared shirt over her bathing suit, her hair damp from swimming, and waving at me to have a putting contest with her on the practice green. So many summer nights, we had putted until the sun had almost vanished. Laughing, needling each other— Davis hated it when she thought I was letting her win—and enjoying each other's company until Mary Alice would yell from the pool that it was time to go home. Thinking back on them now, those days were probably the happiest of my adult life.

As my par putt on seventeen found the bottom of the cup, I felt tears forming in my eyes.

My life is over.

THE EIGHTEENTH HOLE OF THE TWICKENHAM COUNTRY CLUB is a dogleg-right par four. Along the entire right side of the hole is a fence, behind which is Memorial Parkway, the main thoroughfare of Huntsville, Alabama. The tee box sits a few feet from the highway, and, over the years, many a swing had been ruined by a passerby yelling "Fore!" or some other pleasantry or obscenity out of his or her car window. The hole is short and, like most of the holes at Twickenham, tight. The proper play is to lace a fairway wood or a long iron down the middle of the fairway, making sure to keep the ball in play. Such a safe shot would leave about 140 yards for the player's second. If a good player were to hit driver off the tee, he would likely go through the fairway and his ball might hit the clubhouse. Of course, missing left, though not ideal, was better than the alternative. If the tee shot went too far right, then the ball would end up on the parkway.

"We need a birdie here to seal the deal," Simpson snapped as I put my ball in the ground. The other two members of the group—Pat Vowell, an automobile dealership owner who played C, and J. P. Boone, a real estate attorney who was our D—both nodded their encouragement. The beauty of Big Team was that even the C and D players typically contributed at least one birdie a round, and Pat and J.P. had already done their part.

Eighteen wasn't a birdie hole, and many a good round was lost on it. However, a birdie on nine or eighteen was worth double the points. The entire match could flip with one score.

After placing my ball on the tee, I gazed down the fairway. As was my routine on eighteen, I'd chosen my trusty Mac-Gregor persimmon-headed four wood. I hit the club about 210 yards, which was the perfect distance to maximize the length of the fairway without going too far. I took a practice swing and gazed out at the four-lane parkway. At five p.m., cars buzzed past every few seconds.

Then I thought of Darby. Two years ago, a few weeks after retiring from the PGA Tour, Darby had come for a short visit. He had a house on the lake in Rogersville, and he was going to treat me to a round at Turtle Point, one of the finest golf courses in the state. But, at my request, he indulged me with a round at Twickenham. I had wanted to invite a few of the Big Team out to watch, but Darby insisted he didn't want any fuss made.

As he was about to hit his shot off the first tee, he had casually asked me what the course record happened to be. When I told him, "Sixty-three," Darby had smiled and then roped a beautiful draw three hundred yards down the middle of the fairway. He had shot twenty-eight on the inward nine, one better than my score today. Eight birdies and one par. The back, while not quite as spectacular, was still amazing. When he came to the eighteenth hole, all he needed was a par to shoot fifty-eight. To my knowledge, fifty-nine was the greatest round in golf history on any course, and my friend was about to break it.

Darby hadn't been nearly as impressed as me. He had looked out at the finishing hole, which confounded the club's members with its tightness and trouble, and laughed. "Randolph, I bet the members love this booby trap." Then, taking his driver, he lined up his body as if he were going to hit a shot directly into the oncoming traffic on Memorial Parkway.

"Darb, what the hell are you doing?"

"Taking the aggressive route," he said. Before I could stop him, he'd launched his shot into the late-afternoon sky. The ball had started on a beeline for the right-hand lane of the highway and then begun a sweeping draw back across the fence and onto the course. When it came to rest, the ball was on the front of the green twenty feet from the cup.

I hadn't known what to say. It was an even gutsier shot than

I had seen Darby hit at Augusta, and if he hadn't pulled it off, he would have blown his record round. Instead, he two-putted for fifty-seven and made me promise to never tell a soul.

"You gonna hit the ball, Clark, or just watch traffic?" Simpson yelled from his cart. Gritting my teeth, I tried to ignore him. Guys like Bland Simpson gave the game of golf a bad name. If he were given a lie detector test, Simpson wouldn't care whether I made birdie or not. If I did, then he would make money. If I didn't, he'd get to see me choke. That was a win-win proposition to Bland, who seemed to care for no one other than himself.

"Why don't you drink another diet beer and shut your mouth," I said, walking back to the cart and replacing my four wood with a driver.

"What are you doing, boy? Throwing the match?" Simpson asked, but I ignored him.

"Hey, I'm talking to you." His voice had started to slur a little from the beer, and I smiled over my shoulder at him, thinking of what Darby had said to me at Augusta.

"Get your camera ready." Then, taking my stance and not giving myself any time to think about it, I aligned my body with Memorial Parkway. "This one's for you, Darb," I whispered, before starting my swing.

I caught the ball flush and saw it take off over the parkway. At its apex, the ball started to curve left and I grinned.

"Well, I'll be dipped in horse manure," Simpson said.

Though we couldn't see where the ball came to rest from the tee box, it was obvious that if it wasn't on the green, then it was very close.

"Great shot, Clark," J.P. said, slapping me on the back. Pat Vowell, who was sharing my cart with me, leaned close when I sat down and whispered, "The old draw over the parkway, huh?" Pat had a dry sense of humor that I enjoyed.

"It seemed like the thing to do," I said, but I felt heat behind my eyes and heard the crack in my voice on the last word.

"Randy, are you okay?" Pat asked, as I put my foot on the gas and the cart left the tee box.

I looked at him and raised my eyebrows. I had never had another player on the Big Team ever appear even the slightest bit concerned about my well-being. There was almost a code among the players to only discuss business, golf, or other superficial matters.

"Fine, Pat," I managed, but I had tears in my eyes now and wiped them. "It's my fortieth birthday. Guess I'm feeling a little nostalgic."

I could feel that he was still watching me, but I didn't say anything else. Finally, he said, "Well, happy birthday. That was the greatest dadgum shot I've ever seen."

The ball ended up a foot off the green. *Not quite up to you, Darb*, I thought, knowing that the result was perfect. I'd often felt that my life paled in comparison to Darby Hays's. But, gazing at my white ball with the word *Titleist* imprinted across the front of it, I didn't feel the usual bitterness at coming up short. I didn't feel anything at all.

Without even bothering to line my shot up, I went up to the ball with my putter. Since there was nothing between my ball and the green but fairway, I decided to putt and take the risk of flubbing a chip out of play. In golfing circles, the shot was known as a "Texas wedge," because players in Texas used it all the time on their tight, flat fairways. I was about fifty feet from the pin, and my playing partners had surrounded the green. They had all played their shots and now it was my turn. I stepped up to the ball and stroked my putt toward the hole.

The ball never veered and dropped solidly into the cup for an eagle two.

J. P. Boone threw his putter up in the air and ran toward me, picking me up into a big bear hug. Behind him, Pat Vowell held his hand out and I slapped him five. "Incredible," he said.

Still standing by the hole, Bland Simpson reached down and picked the ball out of the cup. I walked toward him, and he flung the Titleist toward me. "Heck of a shot, Clark. You just made us all a boatload of money."

"You're welcome," I said, knowing that the payoff wouldn't even make a dent in the pile of debt that loomed over my family. Shaking my head at the thought, I looked beyond the flag to Memorial Parkway and wondered if Darby Hays had had anything to do with my ball finding the cup.

$$5$$

I DIDN'T GET HOME UNTIL TEN THAT NIGHT. I FELT GUILTY missing my birthday dinner with Mary Alice and Davis, but I couldn't bring myself to go home. For a few fleeting hours, I had escaped the demons of debt and loss that had pounded me into submission these last three years.

After the round had ended, we counted our winnings, which turned out to be five hundred dollars apiece. *Less than a dent*, I had thought, snorting as I put the bills in my pocket. Moq, Mule, Coach, and Finger, who were Big Team staples and had never been taken to the cleaners so bad, stuck around and enjoyed drinks on us. With the eagle on the last, I ended up shooting thirty-four on the back, which, together with my twenty-nine on the front, meant I had tied the course record of sixty-three. According to Bland Simpson, that meant I had to buy all of them a shot of Jack Daniel's, which I did with my winnings.

After golf and drinks was the card game, which sometimes was even more competitive than the golf. But, given all the gin and now whiskey I had consumed, I was having a hard time keeping my eyes open. I said my good-byes after the third hour of poker and trudged to my car, noticing that the full moon above had shone its light over the first fairway. I paused for a moment, marveling at the beauty of the scene, and thought I saw a shadow of a man in the area spotlighted by the moon. I blinked, and the image was gone, but, in my mind's eye, I could still see it. About three hundred yards from the tee, hitting a punch shot toward the green. *Was it Darby or am I just drunk?* I wondered.

As I climbed into the car, my eyes held on the practice green, which was also illuminated by the moon. I pictured my daughter's wet hair and the fierce determination in her eyes as she prepared to putt for the win. And then . . . the sheer joy in her squeal when her ball dropped in the hole.

Daddy, I beat you!

I nodded at the green and put the vehicle in gear.

I HAD NO BUSINESS DRIVING HOME, BUT, MAKING SURE TO stay under the speed limit, I navigated the five miles to our house in the Blossomwood area of Huntsville. We lived in a three-bedroom, two-bathroom house on Locust Avenue. At 2,200 square feet, the home was plenty big enough for the three of us. Once, there had been hopes for at least three kids, a huge house, and perhaps even a lake home or beach condo down the line.

As I pulled into the carport, I could hear the sound of my teeth grinding. Life . . . *and my father* . . . had suffocated our hopes and dreams. After Davis's birth, it had taken us seven years to get pregnant with Graham. When we finally did, Mary

Alice had to have a C-section during delivery and there had been complications. Our son survived his birth, but my wife couldn't have any more children.

And then Graham . . .

I closed my eyes and leaned my forehead on the steering wheel. In my mind, I saw him on Christmas morning three and a half years ago, opening his box of Hot Wheels toy cars and wearing out the rug in the den playing with them all day until he finally fell asleep in his pajamas under the tree. He had been four years old. Dirty-blond hair, brown eyes like his mother, and strong and athletic for his age. He could already throw and catch a baseball and he loved to swing his sister's hand-me-down golf clubs in the backyard. My plan had been to start taking him to the course that summer.

But two weeks after Christmas, he was diagnosed with leukemia. And three months after that, on March 3, just a couple of weeks after his fifth birthday, he was dead.

I squeezed my eyes shut tight, but the tears came all the same. It was thirty-seven months and six days since my son's death. But the pain was still fresh.

A wound that never heals. *Ever* . . .

Finally, I sighed and opened my eyes. I leaned back in the seat and swiped at the moisture that had formed on my cheek. At one point, a year after Graham died, Mary Alice and I had talked of adoption, but neither of us could ever get serious about the proposition.

As for the bigger house and lake property, it was a pipe dream for an insurance defense lawyer. About four years ago, before Graham got sick, I had entertained an offer to join a plaintiff's firm, which offered the possibility of a huge contingency fee, but Dad talked me out of it. *Too much risk for too little reward. For every one winner, there are probably ten guys that lose their butt. It's not worth it, Randy. You have responsibilities . . .*

Though he hadn't said it, I had also heard Dad's general theme when it came to my future: *There comes a point in every man's life when he realizes that he's not going to be Joe Namath.*

So, I had let it go. Then Graham had gotten sick. My health insurance hadn't covered all the bills, and I lost my butt anyway.

Finally, tired of the tortuous trip down memory lane, I stumbled out of my car.

As I entered the home I'd lived in for the past twelve years, I smelled the vague scent of roast beef coming from the kitchen. The only light on in the house came from the television in the den, and I walked toward it. Guilt came back full force. The glow from the tube illuminated the kitchen table, and I saw a birthday cake with forty candles. Next to it was a plate of food that had been covered by a paper towel. I removed the towel and saw my favorite meal. Prime rib and baked potato from Boots' Steakhouse. *She must have gotten it to go . . .* Chagrined, I poured myself a glass of water and walked into the den.

My daughter, Davis, was lying on the couch, her eyes focused on the television set. Her brown hair was still damp from a shower, and she wore a red *Huntsville High Golf* sweatshirt over gray athletic shorts. For the briefest of moments, I caught a glimpse of the eight-year-old girl who had begged me to have putting contests with her in the focused gaze of the sixteen-year-old woman in front of me.

"Hey, Dad," she said, standing and swiping the bangs out of her eyes, which were now etched with worry. "Happy birthday."

"Thanks," I said, pulling her in for a hug. "I'm sorry I missed dinner."

"It's okay, Mom told me about Mr. Hays. I'm so sorry. I always liked him," she said, stepping back from me and crossing her arms.

"He liked you too, champ."

Davis had played golf with Darby and me on several occasions, and two years earlier, Darb had gotten the whole family Masters badges. Walking the hallowed grounds of Augusta National with my wife and daughter was probably the best family moment we had experienced since Graham's death.

"You smell funny. Are you . . . drunk?" She sat back down on the edge of the couch, but her gaze was still fixed on me.

I grunted and then nodded, my cheeks flushing with shame. "Maybe a little."

I plopped down in my brown leather chair next to the couch. On the set was the familiar sight of Augusta National Golf Club, home of the Masters golf tournament. "So what are the talking heads saying?" I asked, hoping to change the subject. One of my and Davis's favorite things to do was to watch ESPN's *SportsCenter* together, where all of the events of the day were wrapped up and highlights were shown.

"Looks like the favorite is Ballesteros, but there are a lot of others that have a chance. Langer, Faldo, Greg Norman . . ." Her voice trailed off.

"Any Americans?"

"Curtis Strange and Tom Kite."

I took a sip of water. "Did they say anything about Jack?"

"No," Davis said. "Only that he's trying out a new putter."

I gave a jerk of my head. I'd seen highlights yesterday of Jack putting on one of the greens with a putter blade that looked twice the size of everyone else's. "When a player starts trying gimmicks . . ." I trailed off.

"They aren't giving him much chance. One reporter said his clubs are 'rusty,' and he should hang them up."

I shook my head at the slight. How could anyone say something like that about the game's greatest champion?

"You should probably check in with Mom," Davis said. "She was pretty upset that you weren't home to go to dinner."

I closed my eyes, remembering the plate of food and cake in the kitchen. "I know," I said, rising from my chair.

"Hey, Dad. Think you'll have time to play eighteen sometime this weekend?"

I gazed down at my daughter, thinking about the plans I had laid for the morning.

"This weekend is going to be tough, champ. I'm sorry."

She looked down at the carpeted floor. "Can we at least watch the final round of the Masters?"

I approached my daughter and leaned down and planted a kiss on the top of her head. "Love you, champ," I said.

She looked up at me. "Love you too, Dad."

Holding back tears, I quickly turned and headed for the kitchen.

"You okay, Dad?" Davis called behind me.

I glanced over my shoulder. "Yeah, hon. Just tired." When I reached our bedroom, I found the door cracked. I peered in and Mary Alice was already asleep. However, as I got closer to the bed, I could hear my wife's sniffles.

"Honey?"

She was lying on her side with her back to me. "Your dinner is on the table. We can eat the cake tomorrow." Her voice was a low whimper, but even through the emotion, I could feel a cold edge to her tone.

"Thank you," I managed. I sat on the bed and placed a hand

on her hip. She didn't turn toward me. "I'm sorry I ruined your plans. The cake looks beautiful."

"Randy?" She looked at me over her shoulder. In the darkness, I couldn't make out her eyes. All I saw was the shadow of her face. "I'm sorry about Darby. I know he was your hero."

I blinked as I gazed at the outline of my wife.

Mary Alice had never cared much for Darby, but she and Charlotte had become close over the years. I opened my mouth to say something comforting, but no words could pass my lips. I patted my wife's hip instead and stood.

She thinks Darby was my hero . . .

As I exited the room, I pictured Darby Hays as I remembered him best. Striding across the thirteenth fairway at Augusta, a cigarette dangling out of the corner of his mouth, winking at me as he went for the green in two. It was true that I had admired the man and envied his accomplishments. *But hero?*

I rested my forehead on the closed bedroom door. "You don't know me at all," I whispered. The words sounded hollow and sad.

Maybe she knows me best of all, I thought, turning around and beginning to trudge back through the house.

I WALKED PAST THE PLATE OF FOOD AND THE BIRTHDAY CAKE with barely a notice, despair overtaking me. Its seed had been planted when I gave up my pursuit of professional golf. Davis's birth and then Graham's and the joy of my family buried it for some time, but when Graham died that seed took root. When Mary Alice and I floundered and then Dad passed on, it flowered. As debt from medical expenses continued to mount over the course of the past year, surpassing two hundred thousand dollars, despair seemed to be all I could feel. Only in fleeting moments with Davis on the golf course, and when I could let loose with Darby, someone I knew who had played the game of life and won, had the despair subsided.

And now Darby Hays was dead. And if I couldn't pay our bills, Davis soon wouldn't be able to play the game we both loved so much.

I'll fix everything tomorrow morning, I thought, envisioning the dark water of the Tennessee River. When I reached the den, Davis was gone. She had left the television on, and the ESPN reporters were still talking about Augusta. I walked over to the bar against the side wall. Not bothering with a glass, I pulled out the bottle of Bombay gin, which I kept only for Darby's visits, and unscrewed the top. I plopped down on the couch and brought the bottle to my lips. As I swallowed, and the heat of the liquor burned my throat, I squinted at the screen. Seve Ballesteros was hitting balls on the driving range. The dashing Spaniard was Mary Alice's favorite golfer, and her infatuation had nothing to do with his golfing ability. The image on the tube shifted to Greg Norman, the Australian golfer whose whitish-blond hair was a stark contrast to Ballesteros. Then Bernhard Langer, the defending champion, was shown walking down one of the holes during his practice round, followed by a split screen of Americans, Tom Kite and Curtis Strange. Finally, Jack Nicklaus was shown. He was also on the practice putting green. When I saw the putter that Davis had mentioned, I could hardly believe my eyes. *A hockey stick*, I thought, taking another swig of gin. As Jack putted, a screen showed a list of all of his accomplishments. Seventeen professional major championships, two U.S. Amateur titles, seventy-two PGA Tour victories, nineteen runner-up finishes in majors, and so on and so forth. Jack's record was both overwhelming and incredible.

But his winning days are numbered, I thought, taking another long swig from the bottle. I again saw the hard surface of the Tennessee River in my mind. I closed my eyes and felt the buzz from the alcohol. I couldn't remember the last time I'd drunk so much in one day. *Probably the beach*, I thought, remembering our last trip to Gulf Shores four years ago.

My mind flashed to images of the sand. Of Davis's jubilant face as she knocked her drive past Darby's on the fourth hole of the Cotton Creek golf course and of Mary Alice's black bikini. Of going up to our room after drinking a couple of Bloody Marys while Darby and Charlotte played in the pool with Graham and Davis. Mary Alice had nodded toward the condo, and a few moments later, we were ripping each other's bathing suits off.

Was that our last time? I wondered, as sleep began to take hold, and I remembered the scents of salt, sex, and vodka mingled with the sounds of the waves and our moans of pleasure. *If it was, we made it count.*

Before I fell asleep, the images picked up speed, moving from the beach with Mary Alice to the ball fields of Little League and the kids. Of showing Davis how to pitch a softball. Of watching her make her first birdie at Twickenham. Of our trip to Disney when Graham was two.

The last image was the one that came every night at some point. Of my boy. My son, Graham Clark, all of five years old. Lying in his bed, wearing his green Incredible Hulk pajamas and gazing up at me with his big brown eyes and asking the type of simple question that had no answers.

"Why did I get cancer, Daddy?"

Why?

Why?

I had no answers then. I have no answers now.

Why?

In my dream, my son's brown eyes eventually turn darker. And then he's gone. And there is only the river. From one hundred feet above.

Cold. Hard. Fast moving.

Why?

6

THE VOICE CAME FROM THE TELEVISION. OR AT LEAST I thought it did.

"I'm not your hero."

I opened my eyes and immediately felt the piercing pain of a hangover hit my temples. The television was still on, but the screen had gone blank. *What time is it?* It had to be three or four in the morning.

"I'm not your hero."

Not the television. Sitting in the leather chair next to me was Darby Hays. He wore a yellow cardigan sweater over a white golf shirt and khaki slacks. *"Darby,"* I whispered, expecting that I would wake up from this dream any minute.

"How do I look, Randolph?" He smiled and, when his mouth creased open, two teeth fell out and hit the ground.

I leaned over the couch to vomit, but instead of the carpeted floor of the den, I spewed on a patch of matted-down weeds and torn branches.

"Gin always made you sick as a dog, Randolph."

I stared at the weeds, coughing and willing myself to wake up. *What is happening?*

Slowly, I rose back to a sitting position. I sat in the passenger side of a convertible sports car. The windshield was cracked, and the smell of fuel was thick in the air.

"I'd probably get out of there if I were you." It was Darby's voice. But from where?

Even though I knew this had to be a dream, I fumbled for the latch. I stepped out of the car and stumbled a few steps away. The ground was uneven, and I heard branches crack as I walked. *Where am I?*

"You're in the woods below Hugh Daniel Drive," Darby's baritone voice blared out. "That's my Jaguar." I peered over my shoulder at the white convertible. "I loved that car," Darby said. Then, I heard him whisper, "Five, four, three . . . step back, Randolph."

I did as he instructed.

". . . one."

The explosion rattled my eardrums, and the woods were now lit up with an orange glow of fire. I gazed past the flames that had engulfed the car and, fifty yards beyond, I saw the asphalt road.

"Were you in the car?" I asked.

"No," Darby fired back. "I was thrown from the Jag when it started tumbling down the hill. I wasn't wearing my seat belt. I was drunk."

"Not smart," I managed, bringing my thumbs to my temples.

"Follow me, Randolph." The baritone voice felt like it was right in my ear, but when I turned, I saw that he was now thirty feet away. Almost out of sight.

"I want to show you something," the ghost of Darby Hays whispered.

This whole thing is impossible, I thought. But, as the darkness closed in and the ghost continued to drift farther into the woods, I felt my feet begin to follow.

"I'm going to give you something."

"What?" I rasped, stumbling over some brush as I tried to catch up.

"A gift," Darby said. "A great and wonderful gift."

7

WHEN I FINALLY CAUGHT UP WITH DARBY, WE STEPPED OUT OF the woods together. It was as if they just fell away. For a brief moment there was darkness, but then, gradually, night began to fade. As sunlight poured into the clearing, I saw that we were standing on the edge of a fairway.

"Recognize this place?" Darby asked, lifting his arm and pointing.

I followed his finger down the tightly manicured grass. About two hundred fifty yards ahead, a creek jutted across the fairway. Beyond the water and up a steep slope of tight grass was the green. I could see the yellow flag, which was tucked on the front right of the green. Behind the putting surface were four bunkers. Between the sand hazards were azaleas in full bloom.

"I have this portrait on my wall at the office." I could hear the shock and awe in my voice. "The thirteenth hole at Augusta."

Darby took several steps toward the center of the fairway

and dropped two golf balls from his pocket. When he turned back around to me, he was holding a persimmon-headed wood in his hand.

I smiled. "I saw you hit this shot in the 1976 Masters."

Darby waggled the club and placed it behind the ball. Then he set his feet and peeked at the green. Without any warning, he began his swing, sweeping the clubhead back and then cocking his wrists. As he turned his left shoulder so that his back was to the target, I saw a tiny grin on his face. For a moment, his body almost seemed to pause before his weight shifted to his left and he unwound his coiled body toward the ball. When the face of the club made contact with the ball, the resulting crack sounded like dynamite. I watched the ball ascend into the air toward the flagstick. When the ball reached its full height, I saw it drift about five yards to the left. My smile widened. *Darby's patented draw.*

For a brief moment, I thought Darby hadn't caught all of it and that the ball would splash into the water. Instead, it landed a couple feet onto the green and about twenty feet from the hole. Then, after taking a couple of short hops, it began to feed to the right, tracking toward the hole.

"There's a speed slope on the green," Darby said. "If you catch the incline, the ball will head to the right." He paused. "They normally put the pin there on Sunday."

I nodded as I thought back to the prior Masters tournaments I had watched. Putting the pin on the front right maximized the chance for a good shot and would tempt many players to go for the green in two. The thirteenth hole was a par five, so hitting the green on his second shot would give the player a chance at an eagle three. Of course, if he came up short, he'd be in the water and likely to make a bogey. That could cost a player a good round. And, on Sunday, the championship. *The Masters doesn't really begin until the back nine on Sunday*, I thought, hearing the familiar refrain that the broadcasters liked to say.

Darby's ball finally came to rest very close to the hole. From two hundred fifty yards out it was hard to tell, but I guessed it was about two feet.

"Great shot," I said. "Do you remember hitting that same shot in the third round of the '76 Masters?"

"I was a little closer to the green in '76."

"It was the best golf shot I've ever seen hit in a tournament."

Darby grimaced. Then he handed me the club. "Here, you try."

I laughed. "Darby, you know I can't hit this shot. I can barely hit a teed-up driver two sixty, and we are at least two fifty from the hole."

"It's the thirteenth hole of Augusta, Randolph, and you're talking to a ghost. Live a little." He pushed the handle of the three wood into my hand.

I took the club and shrugged. On a good day, I could hit my three wood about two hundred forty yards, so I figured I was ten yards out of my range. *But if I catch it just right . . .* Just then, I felt a slight breeze behind me that hadn't been present before.

Without thinking about it, I stepped toward the ball and set the clubhead behind it. I took my stance, lining up slightly to the right of the flag. My only chance was to hit a sweeping draw. I looked one last time at the green, then began my swing. The club felt light in my hand and, surprisingly, my body was loose and nimble. When I connected with the ball, I knew I had hit it pure.

"That-a-boy, Randolph," Darby said.

I began to walk after the ball, trying to will it across Rae's

Creek. *I've wanted to hit that shot my whole life*, I thought, peering at the ball and knowing that I had stepped directly into the portrait that adorned my office wall. I held my breath and waited as the ball reached its apex and began to curve to the left.

"You're home," Darby said, before the ball landed.

And he was right. It cleared the creek by a couple yards and came to rest about thirty feet to the left of the flag.

"Didn't hit the speed slope, though," Darby said. "But still not bad."

"That was the best shot I've ever hit," I whispered.

"No, it wasn't," Darby snapped, beginning to stride toward the green.

"What do you mean?" I asked, following after him and taking in the surreal scene of me, Randy Clark, walking down the thirteenth hole of Augusta National Golf Club.

"I mean that wasn't the best shot you've ever hit. Hell, I've seen you hit one a lot better than that."

I snorted. "Like when?"

"Remember that pro-am at Shoal Creek four years ago? We had a Nassau bet with Jerry Pate's group. We had it in the bag, but we needed you to knock your shot on the green on the seventeenth hole. You had 148 yards, slight wind in your face, and two professional golfers watching you, not to mention six amateurs who probably all hoped you'd peel sod and dump it in the drink."

"That was just a seven iron, Darb."

He came to a dead stop and stuck his finger in my chest. "A seven iron you hit when you had to make the shot. A seven iron that landed ten feet from the flag and guaranteed us the victory."

"How in the world do you remember that?"

Darby grinned, and I noticed the missing teeth in his mouth. "I'm a ghost now, Randolph. I've been sent here to show you something, and I remember things that maybe you should remember. That was a great shot hit under pressure when you had to have it." He paused and then winked. "The drive you hit today on the eighteenth hole at Twickenham out over the parkway and the eagle putt you drained were both pretty frisky too."

I studied him. "Did you have anything to do with that putt dropping?"

He shook his head. "No, sirree. That was all you."

I scratched the back of my neck and sighed. "None of the shots of mine you've mentioned were even close to your three wood on this hole . . ." I stopped and waved my hand at the beautiful scenery that surrounded us in every direction. "That was a major championship."

He smiled, but his sunken eyes were sad. "Yeah, I hit that shot. You remember the putt for eagle?"

"Well . . . as I recollect, you two-putted for birdie."

"I missed a five-foot putt for eagle that would have gotten me within two of Watson and Crenshaw. The ball didn't even scare the hole, and I barely made the comebacker. I didn't sniff a birdie the rest of the way and I shot seventy-eight the next day to not even make the top twenty."

I glared at him. "You played the tour for nineteen years. You made hundreds of thousands of dollars. You won four PGA Tour events."

"Five," Darby corrected.

"Exactly. *Five*. You played the Masters almost twenty times." I again waved my hand behind me and breathed in the scent of the Georgia pines that lined both sides of the fairway.

"I never won a major. I never played in the Ryder Cup." Darby sighed. "And by the time I retired, I had blown every cent I ever made on a golf course." He snickered. "When my Jaguar ran off the road early yesterday morning, the only money I had in the bank came from my dealerships."

We crossed the small footbridge that took us over Rae's Creek. "You lived my dream, Darb. You played the finest courses. You walked alongside Jack Nicklaus and Arnold Palmer and Tom Watson. I've looked up to you my whole life." I paused in the middle of the bridge. "Hell, I guess Mary Alice was right. You are my hero."

Darby stopped and wheeled on me. "No, I'm not. I'm a drunk. I was a poor husband and an even worse friend."

"Are you kidding? You got me Masters badges every year."

Darby shook his head and dropped the club from his hands. The sky had become darker and I couldn't see the green anymore. I felt dizzy. I leaned over the railing, but I didn't see Rae's Creek anymore.

Instead, I saw the muddy water of the Tennessee River. I was standing in the same spot where I had stood when my birthday had begun. The place where I planned to jump and end my life.

"Where was I when you lost Graham?" Darby asked. His voice was in my ear, but I couldn't see him. "Did I come to the hospital? Did I even make the funeral?"

"I didn't hold that against you," I said, closing my eyes. I squeezed them tight, but then, as if by some sort of magnetic pull, I felt my lids opening. I now heard the beeps of the monitors and the sound of sniffling. Mary Alice sat on the bed, rubbing my boy's forehead, whispering, "It's okay to let go, baby boy." By the window, my mother's angelic face was streaked with tears. She had her arm wrapped around Davis, who had buried her face in her chest. Davis had been twelve.

I saw myself standing by my son's bed. I heard the sound of the monitor as the line on the screen went flat. There was a long monotone beep. I heard my wife's shriek and saw my hands go to my knees.

"Darby, get me out of here," I said. I turned away from the awful scene and saw my father. He leaned his back against the far wall of the hospital room. His arms were crossed, and a tear streaked his cheek. I don't remember seeing Dad when Graham died. I knew he was there, but everything was a blur. I could see him now.

I turned back to the bed, but I was no longer in the hospital. Now I was at Maple Hill Cemetery.

Though the visitation the day before had been huge and overwhelming, the graveside service was small. Only family and close friends.

As I approached the tent, I saw myself standing by the casket. Behind me, Mary Alice sat stoically in her chair in the front row. Tears had smeared her makeup, but she took no notice. Davis and my mother sat next to her.

My father stood behind me and whispered something in my ear.

"What did he say?" Darby asked.

I turned and saw that my friend was standing beside me. "That I needed to be strong. That Davis would look to me to be the example. That Mary Alice would need me too." I sighed. "Stuff I already knew."

"I should have been here," Darby said.

"Where were you?"

Darby grimaced and snapped his fingers. When he did, the

cemetery evaporated. I wiped my eyes as they adjusted to the new scene. We were standing in a dank hotel room. The carpet was greenish brown. The covers had been thrown off the king-sized bed, and Darby lay sprawled in the middle of it. There was an empty bottle of gin on the bedside table. Beside the liquor was a tin plate with a white powdery substance smeared all over it.

I turned and saw a woman emerge from the bathroom. She had just showered, and her body was barely covered by a towel. Beautiful. Sexy. And not Charlotte.

I watched her glide into the room and look at Darby's body on the bed. Then, shaking her head, she went over to the couch, where Darby's pants had been flung, and she pulled his wallet out of the back pocket. I watched her take at least five bills out of it, and then, without even a glance at Darby, she got dressed and walked out of the room.

"Cold," I said.

"Want to know how many times that scene played out in nineteen years?"

"No," I said, feeling a wave of depression come over me.

"I missed your son's funeral because I was in the middle of the Florida swing on tour. I could have flown to Huntsville, but I didn't."

"You were a professional golfer. You were working."

"That look like work?" Darby asked, his voice sick with sarcasm, as he pointed at himself on the bed. I glanced at Darby, expecting to see the old mischievous grin with a wink thrown in, but he gazed back at me with blank eyes. Dead eyes.

"I didn't have a life, Randolph. I never had children. I was a terrible friend. An even worse husband, and my reckless life got me killed last night." He snapped his fingers, and in an instant, I was back on the Tennessee River Bridge.

"But you do have a life, Randy."

I felt my heartbeat speed up as I turned to my friend. I couldn't remember the last time he had called me "Randy."

"You were everything I ever wanted to be, Darb."

"No, I wasn't," he snapped. "You didn't want to be me, and I darn sure wasn't your hero."

Glancing down at the dark current and then back to the ghost of Darby Hays, I whispered, "What are we doing? Why are you here?"

He stepped closer to me.

"Before I leave you and this world forever, I need to tell you about the gift you are about to receive."

"Gift?"

He nodded. "You see, Randolph, you have had heroes, just not me." He paused. "And you are going to have the opportunity to play a round of golf or . . . something like that . . . with each of them. Four heroes. Four rounds. A tournament, so to speak, with the champions you've looked up to your whole life." He chuckled. "The Randy Clark Invitational."

"Why?" I asked. It was the only thing I could think to say.

Now, Darby did give me his trademark smile of mischief followed by a wink. "You'll see, old friend." He began to walk away, and I ran after him. In the distance, I saw an eighteen-wheeler approaching.

"What am I supposed to get from this?" I asked, trying to catch up to my friend but losing ground. The roar of the tractor-trailer's engine was closer, and Darby was walking straight for it. "Darb!" I ran toward him, but it was no use. When the rig was a few feet away from him, Darby turned to face me.

"I'm sorry, Randolph. For everything."

"No!" I screamed, trying to run but unable to move my

feet. The rig passed right through Darby as if he weren't there. Now, it headed straight for me. Again, I tried to move my feet, but it was no use.

As the grille of the truck came into focus, I saw a man behind the wheel. I gaped at the figure. For a moment, I couldn't make him out, but then his eyes seemed to glow. My father leaned his head over the wheel.

"There comes a point in every man's life when he realizes that he's not going to be Joe Namath."

The voice was then drowned out by the sound of the engine, and headlights flashed in my eyes.

I tried to scream, but no words would come. I covered my face with my hands and dropped to my knees, squeezing my eyes shut. As my nostrils filled with the scent of diesel fuel, my vocal cords finally let loose.

And I screamed at the top of my lungs.

FIRST ROUND

8

WHEN MY EYES FLEW OPEN, IT WASN'T AN EIGHTEEN-WHEELER driven by my father that I saw. It was my daughter, Davis, crouching over me with a terrified expression on her face.

"Dad! Wake up! Dad!"

I was lying on the carpeted floor of the den. "Davis?"

"Yeah," she said. Her eyes were creased with concern. "You were having a nightmare. A bad one."

I sat up and grabbed hold of my knees. My head was pounding with a horrific headache. Funny, the pain from the hangover had gone away when I had started talking to Darby in the dream, but now it was back with a vengeance. "Can you get me some water, champ?"

"Okay," Davis said, her voice wary as she rose and started walking toward the kitchen.

"Randy?" Mary Alice asked, brushing past our daughter and stopping when she saw me on the floor.

"Nightmare," I said.

She folded her arms across her chest. She was wearing a

white bathrobe that she had tied in front. He hair was matted down on the side she had slept on and a strand was hanging in her face. Her eyes were puffy from sleep and her face was pale. Still, she looked beautiful as the sun shone through the cracked blinds of the den onto her face.

I managed to stand and felt piercing daggers of pain in my temples. Davis returned with a glass of ice water, and I took a long sip. I looked around the den and saw the bottle of gin on the coffee table. The top was still off. Shame poured through me at being found by Davis like this. Then I felt a soft touch on my arm.

"Was your dream about Graham?"

I looked into Mary Alice's kind brown eyes and past her to Davis, whose face was stoic. I rubbed the back of my neck, knowing that my dream had gone far beyond Graham. *But he had been a part of it*, I thought, remembering the sight of my father leaning against the far wall of the hospital room.

I nodded.

Her eyes glistened, and she wrapped her arms around me. "How do you feel?"

I snorted. "Hungover." I pulled back from her. "I'm so sorry I missed dinner last night."

She squeezed my arms. "It's okay. I told you to take the day off. I'm sorry about Darby."

My body tensed as I heard my friend's name, and a vision of his ghost popped into my head. The teeth falling out of his mouth when he had grinned.

"What time is it?"

"Six thirty in the morning," Davis said. "Your yelling cheated me out of fifteen minutes of sleep."

"Sorry," I said, taking another drink of water.

Mary Alice turned and began to walk toward the kitchen. "How about some coffee?"

"Sounds good," I managed. As my bearings returned to me, I sat heavily in one of the chairs at the kitchen table. The cake with its forty candles still adorned the center. It had a plastic covering to keep it fresh.

"Maybe we can celebrate your birthday tonight," Mary Alice said, as she put a coffee filter in the maker.

"Okay," I said, knowing that if everything went as planned, Mary Alice would likely be at a funeral home tonight tending to my arrangements.

As I watched my wife effortlessly move about the kitchen, I heard the sound of the shower crank up in the back. Davis had started to get ready for school. I took another gulp from the glass and my thoughts drifted back to the dream. Darby Hays sitting in my leather chair in the den. Then me in the passenger side of Darby's Jaguar at the crash site. The explosion. Then the thirteenth hole at Augusta. Walking over the footbridge of Rae's Creek, which had turned into the Tennessee River Bridge. Then the hospital room. The cemetery. The hotel room. The images flashed through my mind like they were on a fast-moving projector screen.

I'm not your hero.

You will be given a great gift.

Four heroes. Four rounds.

The Randy Clark Invitational.

I drained the rest of the water. When I stood from the chair, my head didn't feel quite as bad, though I was still woozy from the dream.

"I'm going to get cleaned up," I said, beginning to walk out of the kitchen.

Her voice stopped me "Randy?"

"Yeah?" I turned and looked at her.

"Are you okay?"

No.

"Fine, hon. Thank you. Just hungover and still in shock over Darby."

Her eyes narrowed. It looked like she was going to add something, but all that came out was "Okay."

9

ON MY WAY TO THE BRIDGE I STOPPED AT GIBSON'S, A BARBE-
cue joint on Memorial Parkway that also served breakfast. I
planned to get a coffee to go, but the smell of biscuits, bacon,
and sausage made my stomach growl. *Even death row inmates get
a last meal*, I thought. I grabbed a booth in the rear, hoping not
to be recognized by anyone, and ordered the works: eggs, bacon, grits, and biscuits and gravy. After a few bites, my stomach
and head began to loosen. *I'm gonna live*, I thought. Then, realizing the absurdity of the thought given what I was planning to
do afterward, I shook my head.

I thought about my visit from Darby.

Four heroes. Four rounds.

You do have a life, Randy.

As I headed toward the cash register, I glanced around the
bustling establishment, seeing groups of middle-aged men and
women talking, laughing, and eating. People *living*.

I paid for the meal and walked briskly toward my car. When
was the last time I had felt *alive*?

I couldn't remember. And, in about an hour, none of it would matter anymore. As I put the key in the ignition, I heard a knock on the window. I turned and almost winced when I saw the familiar face.

"Randy Clark!"

I tried hard not to sigh as I rolled the window down. "Hey, Mick. How you doing?"

White-haired and besuited, Mickey Spann had sold life insurance for the past forty years. "Randy, I've been trying to reach you. Is your secretary not giving you my messages?"

"I'm sorry, Mick. Just been busy lately."

Mickey shook his head, but the ever-present grin on his face only widened. "So much like your father. Robert worked like a dog every day of his life." He paused. "But when he passed, he'd let me set him up so that your momma was taken care of."

"Mickey, I have the maximum term coverage. I couldn't get more protection for Mary Alice and Davis even if I wanted to, right?"

The salesman had a twinkle in his eye. "The company has a new product that would be perfect for you. Permanent coverage that would actually pay a return." He shrugged. "You'd have to pay a little more now, but you'd start earning interest. Term coverage is great, Randy, but a man of your means needs more."

A man of my means? I owe a quarter of a million dollars to the hospital in unpaid bills for Graham.

When I didn't answer, Mickey reached through the window to put a hand on my shoulder. "Look, I know you've had a tough go of it with your son and then your dad. Your father and I were good friends for thirty years, and there's not a day that goes by that I don't think of him."

I pictured Dad from my dream the night before. Leaning his head over the steering wheel of the rig. "Me too, Mick."

"Your father sure would be proud of you," he said.

"If you say so," I said. I started to roll up the window, but Mickey stuck his hand in the opening to block it. "Mick, I need—"

"He would be," Mickey said, his voice firm. I had rarely if ever heard anger creep into Mickey Spann's voice, but there was a twinge of it in his tone now. I looked up at the man, who had to be at least eighty-five years old. Long past retirement age, but still peddling life insurance as if every customer might be his last. "One of the last times I saw him, when hospice had come into his and your mom's house, he told me something that I want you to hear."

I sighed. "What?"

"That he didn't think he'd been a great father."

I almost laughed, but held it in. "Really?"

Mickey nodded. "Said he had been too harsh. Not enough hugs." His face curved into a sad smile. "I'm a Stephen Minister at the church, and I hear that a lot from people, especially older men who regret not being better to their children. He said he had tried to do well by you, but that he didn't think you knew how much he respected you." Mick's voice began to shake with emotion. "How much he loved you."

I felt heat behind my own eyes. It was hard to imagine my father saying anything like that.

I didn't know what to say, so I just nodded at Mick.

"You have a valuable life, Randy. A good and valuable life." The glint was back in his eye. "Let's do lunch on Monday, what do you say? A meat and three and let me tell you about this product." He held out his hand and I took it.

"Sounds good, Mick."

He gave my hand a squeeze. "Good man." He began to walk away, but then he stopped and gazed back at me over his shoulder. "Remember what I said about your daddy, son."

I gave him a nod. "Will do."

10

I LEFT GIBSON'S IN A FOG. THE IRONY OF BUMPING INTO Mickey Spann wasn't lost on me. Here I was about to take my own life, and the insurance policy that I had purchased from Mickey was what I was relying on to take care of my family. It was a three-million-dollar policy with no exclusion for suicide after the expiration of five years. I had bought it seven years earlier, not thinking that I might one day try to take advantage of any loopholes. But a few months ago, after receiving another demand letter from the hospital and then having my first consultation with a bankruptcy attorney, I reviewed the policy with a fine-toothed comb and even suffered through a lunch with Mickey to "better understand what I had." I had innocently asked about the exclusions that were still applicable, and Mickey had confirmed that "not even suicide was excluded anymore."

Mary Alice will be able to pay off Graham's medical expenses and still have more than enough to live on.

I pulled onto Memorial Parkway. I passed the turn for

downtown, which would have taken me to my office. I felt my heart rate speed up as my decision solidified. Darby Hays was dead, and I planned to join him in just under an hour. I turned left onto Highway 72 and squeezed tight to the wheel, fighting off the doubts the dream had caused.

You do have a life, Randy.

"No, I don't," I said out loud, beating the wheel with my fist. What would my death do to Davis? Would she be able to handle it? Davis and I had been as close as a father and daughter could be before Graham's death, but nothing had been the same since. Now that she was driving a car, we hardly ever spent any time together.

I've got no money socked away for her college. I spent every dime on Graham's medical care. Davis is a good student and a talented golfer, but getting an academic or athletic scholarship is a long shot. College will be too unless . . .

". . . unless I jump," I said, my voice firm as I nodded at the windshield. When I did the math and analyzed my options, I always came up with the same conclusion. *This is the only way I can help my daughter. She'll have money for college. Her future will be ahead of her.*

Up ahead, the traffic was beginning to slow. *What now?* As the traffic came to a stop I pulled onto the shoulder and continued driving, anxious to follow through on my plan. A hundred yards up, I saw an orange detour sign. Beyond the sign, I saw what had stopped traffic. There had been a wreck in the intersection of Highway 72 and Jeff Road. A storage truck had T-boned what looked like a Cadillac sedan. When I reached the detour sign, I turned right onto Jeff Road. There was another sign ahead and, without thinking about it any further, I followed. *Why isn't anyone else taking the detour?*

I scratched my head and felt my heart starting to pound. *What the . . .*

The end of the detour was a parking lot with a mobile home that sat where asphalt met grass. Adjacent to the trailer were a number of golf carts lined up. *Why would there be a detour to the old Monrovia Golf Course?* I wondered, easing the car to a stop. When I did, I saw a woman emerge from the trailer. She had long blond hair and wore green shorts and a yellow golf shirt. She smiled as she approached, and I rolled down the window.

"There are some balls on the range for you to warm up with, Mr. Clark."

Balls? Range? As far as I could remember, the old Monrovia Golf Course didn't have a driving range. The course was a municipal track that was home to the cheapest golf in town.

"There must be some mistake," I managed, squinting up into her bluish-green eyes. "I'm not playing golf today. I don't even have my clubs."

"No mistake, Mr. Clark. We got a call about fifteen minutes ago from your friend, Mr. Hays, that you would be arriving at eight thirty a.m."

I felt my heart constrict. *Mr. Hays . . .*

"That's impossible," I said.

"Not at all," the woman said, walking behind my vehicle to the trunk. She opened it, and sure enough, there was my golf bag.

Gooseflesh now covered every square inch of my body. I glanced at my arms, and I was no longer wearing a button-down shirt. Instead, I had on a blue sweater. I didn't have to check my collar to know that I was now wearing a golf shirt.

"Want to change into your spikes here or in the locker room?"

I gazed past her to the trailer. *Locker room?* "Here," I managed.

"Okay, suit yourself," she said, throwing my golf bag over her shoulder. "I'll put these on the range. Your playing partner is already here."

"My playing . . . partner?" I asked, opening the door to the Crown Vic and stepping out of it on shaking legs.

She flung her hair back and peered at me over her shoulder. "Yes. Mr. Bob."

My eyes widened, but I didn't say anything else. I walked around to my trunk and took my time slipping my golf shoes on. Then, taking in a deep breath, I ambled toward the trailer. As I walked, I noticed there were no other cars in the lot and, looking past the trailer, no golfers on the course. I didn't see a driving range anywhere.

Darb, what have you gotten me into? I whispered, as I grabbed the knob. Then, too bewildered to think about it any longer, I opened the door and stepped inside.

11

"OH . . . MY . . . GOD." I SPOKE MY THOUGHTS ALOUD AS I gawked up and around at the richly adorned clubhouse. Portraits of old men, some in golf attire and others wearing a coat and tie, lined all four walls of the mammoth building. There was a chandelier that hung from the tall ceiling and a twisting staircase that led to a second floor. The smell of strong coffee and pastries hung in the air, and I noticed several men sitting around tables in the nineteenth-hole lounge just ahead of where I was standing.

There were few truths in an uncertain world, but this was one of them—I was not inside the trailer of the old Monrovia Golf Course.

I felt a hand touch my arm, and I turned to see a man wearing a brown suit, white shirt, and tie. Round glasses perched on his nose, and he had a thatch of neatly cut salt-and-pepper hair. "You're all set up on the range, Mr. Clark. Follow me, sir."

Swallowing hard, I did as I was told, maneuvering through the lounge and the golf shop and finally out onto a veranda. I sucked in a breath as I took in the golf course in front of me. Tree-lined fairways. Grass as "green as goose dung," Darby would say. I saw an area where a man appeared to be hitting balls by himself. "Is that—?"

"Yes, sir," the man wearing the brown suit said, gesturing for me to continue to follow. I walked behind him down a long brick staircase and out into the sunshine. When the rays hit my face, I felt an almost giddy sensation, reminding me of the summer days when my mom would drop me off in the morning at Twickenham. The golf team got the run of the club during the summer, and I was the team's A player. I'd play thirty-six holes a day and hit two hundred balls and never get tired. In the dog days of late July, I'd take a dip in the swimming pool after each round.

I breathed in the fresh air and smiled at the memory. Then reality gripped me for a second. *Where am I and what in the world am I doing?*

As I followed the man, I remembered Darby's words.

Four heroes. Four rounds. A tournament, so to speak, with the champions you've looked up to your whole life . . .

As I continued to walk toward the range, I glanced back at the clubhouse and felt my stomach tighten. I stopped and gaped at the backside of the Tudor building, marveling at the architecture. I had been here before. I knew this place. *Four heroes. Four rounds . . .*

When it came to me, I gasped out loud.

"East Lake," I whispered. Darby had lined up a round for us about ten years ago.

"Yes," the man with the brown suit said back, also whispering. I looked at him again, thinking about all the stories I'd heard about the boy who grew up playing here. The boy who would become one of golf's greatest champions. Perhaps the sport's first icon. I gazed at the old man again and saw the notebook he held in his hand.

"You're Mr. Keeler, aren't you? O. B. Keeler?"

The man smiled. "You need to warm up, sir?"

"It *is* you," I said in awe. I spun around and gazed at the lone golfer hitting balls on the range. The man wore knickers, but he did not have on a cap or a hat. Even from twenty yards away, I recognized the long fluid motion of his swing. The sound of the crack when the clubhead connected with the ball resembled a gunshot.

"Bobby Jones," I whispered again, feeling my heartbeat racing.

I felt a nudge on my back and looked at the brown-suited man. O. B. Keeler had been Bobby Jones's personal chronicler, a newspaperman who followed Jones to all of his many tournaments and summarized his greatest victories and most difficult defeats. He'd written several biographies on Jones and was probably the person who knew the great champion the best. "Go on," he said.

Forcing my legs, which were now shaking, to move, I walked toward the range. I saw my own golf bag a few feet away from Jones's and almost laughed at the absurdity of the picture. Jones's signless tote bag with the ancient hickory-shafted tools inside contrasted with my bright red bag with the word *Titleist* embroidered in white down the side. I had steel-shafted irons and woods.

"Mr. Clark?"

I turned back to Keeler, whose friendly demeanor had turned serious. "Do pay attention."

Puzzled, I managed to nod. I started to walk toward the range again and Keeler disappeared.

Where did he go? Moving my head around the historic grounds and clubhouse, I saw no one else.

"It's just us now." The voice dripped with southern elegance. It was the accent I'd heard on old telecasts of the Masters and on a VHS tape of golf lessons the legend had once done with actor W. C. Fields.

"Mr. Jones?" I asked, moving toward him.

He smiled and stared back at the driving range, waggling what looked like a mid-iron in his hand. He kicked his right knee toward his left to start his swing, and then I watched as the only man to ever win golf's Grand Slam launched a shot high into the air.

"Nice shot," I said.

"Caught it a little thin, but it will work." He reached into his pants and brought out a cigarette. Lighting it with a match, he breathed a smoke cloud in the air. "Hit you a few balls, Randy, and I'll see you on the first tee, okay? Johnnie will be over in a minute to get our bags."

"O-O-Okay," I stammered, watching him glide away toward a tee box in the distance.

Darby, what in God's name have you gotten me into? I thought again.

"I'd start with a few wedges, and then work my way up to the driver," a man with a Scottish accent said, and I turned toward the sound. Leaning against a water jug was a small, stout man wearing a black ivy hat and white knickers. "Or you can hit whatever ye like."

I grabbed a wedge from the bag and took a couple of practice swings. My legs still felt rubbery from shock. *When am I gonna wake up?* I wondered, putting my club behind the ball and promptly blading my first shot out onto the range. I felt heat on my cheeks as I brushed another ball out of the bucket. My next shot was a cold chunk. I hit almost a foot behind the ball and the shot barely went fifteen yards. My face was now throbbing with embarrassment, and I didn't dare look up. I brought another ball over and loosened my grip pressure, focusing on keeping my head steady. This time, I made solid contact and the ball climbed into the air and dropped out into the middle of the range, about one hundred twenty yards out.

"There eet is," the Scotsman said from behind me. "Nice fluid move, Mr. Clark."

"Thank you," I managed, beginning to relax as I struck another pure wedge. I hit two more wedge shots and about four seven irons, then grabbed the driver. I addressed the ball, playing it up in my stance, and tried to emulate the swing of Bobby Jones. *Soft and smooth*, I whispered. The ball launched off the face like a rocket, and I knew I couldn't hit one any better.

"I'd save the rest of those for the course," Johnnie said, already moving toward me to take the club.

"Good idea," I said.

Despite carrying both bags, Johnnie walked at a brisk pace that was hard to keep up with. By the time I reached the first tee, which was about a hundred yards away, I was almost out of breath.

My playing partner sat on a bench with one leg crossed over the other. He was smoking a cigarette. His pants were knickers and he wore a shirt and tie, which I knew was the dress of most accomplished golfers back in the twenties and thirties.

"Mr. Jones, it is an honor to play with you."

He rose from his seat and flicked the cigarette on the grass, quickly stomping it out with his spikes. "The pleasure is all mine, Randy. Call me Bob, okay?"

I nodded, feeling butterflies in my stomach. *How does he know me?* It was all so surreal, as I heard Darby's voice again in my mind.

Four heroes. Four rounds . . .

"How does your head feel, Randy?" Bob said, as he took the driver that Johnnie had already pulled out of his bag for him to hit. He smiled at me and then walked onto the tee box of the first hole at East Lake.

"My head?" I asked, taking my own driver from Johnnie and gazing at the legend who was now sizing up his first tee shot.

Bob chuckled. "You drank enough to down three men yesterday."

I felt my cheeks flush with embarrassment. But before I could respond, Bob launched his drive down the fairway. It was, as I would expect, a beautiful golf shot carrying at least two hundred seventy yards on the fly.

"Nice shot," Johnnie called out.

Bob glanced at me. "This is a four-hundred-yard par four. Slightly uphill. Nice and straight hole to start with."

"I know," I told him, walking around him and putting my tee in the ground. "I've played East Lake before."

Feeling adrenaline flooding my veins, I aligned my body parallel to the fairway and, without further thought, swung the club. I knew I had flushed it the minute the head of the club hit the ball, and I held my follow-through as the ball climbed into the air. I couldn't tell where it ended up, but my guess was that I was at least close to Jones.

"Nice one," Bob said.

"Very nice indeed," Johnnie said, taking the club from me and beginning to churn his legs down the fairway.

As I began to walk side by side with the great champion, I spoke without looking at him. "How did you know about what I drank?"

I felt a strong hand clasp my back and give it a squeeze. "I know everything about you, Randy. We all do."

"We . . . all?"

"Four rounds, remember?"

Four rounds. Four heroes, I thought, nodding at him.

"Randy Clark," Bob said, speaking in a lower tone. "Second place, 1968 Alabama State Amateur. Played number one on the Alabama golf team in the late 1960s. Tried to make the tour but missed getting through Q school by a single stroke. Girlfriend Mary Alice got pregnant and Randy gave up his dream of being a golfer and went to law school. Became a lawyer in Huntsville, Alabama. Developed an insurance defense practice." Bob paused. "You know, I was a lawyer once."

I smiled at him. "You wanted to go into trial law, right?"

"I did, but then in one of my first trials, the judge on the case asked to play golf with me and started giving me favorable rulings." He shook his head. "I never wanted any favoritism. If it wasn't going to be pure, I wanted none of it, so I stayed out of the courtroom from then on."

"You were the greatest golfer that ever lived . . . I mean, you know . . ." I began to fumble my words as I realized what I was about to say.

Bob laughed out loud. "You mean until Jack came along."

"You both are incredible players."

He nodded. "I once said that Jack Nicklaus played a game unfamiliar to me, and I meant it. He hits the ball farther and straighter than any player before or since."

"He's pretty much done now," I said.

"That so?" Bob said. "He's playing in my tournament this week, isn't he?"

I smiled, knowing that Bobby Jones, along with Clifford Roberts, had founded the Masters golf tournament. "Jack is in the field, but most folks aren't giving him much of a shot."

"What do you think, Randy?"

I sighed as we reached our golf balls in the fairway. "He'll never be what he once was."

"Are any of us?" Bob asked.

I peered at him, but he was not looking at me. Instead, he was gazing ahead at the green. "What do we have here, Johnnie? One forty?"

"Aye," the Scotsman said. "One thirty-eight for you, sir, and Mr. Clark has 141. We are going uphill a bit, so you may want to take a little more club."

"Hand me the nine iron," Bob said.

I looked at the green. That was probably the right club for the yardage. But with the incline, I knew I needed more club. "Me too," I said.

"Aye," Johnnie said, handing me the club. "You have the honors, Mr. Clark."

"Thanks," I snapped, knowing I shouldn't be the least bit angry that Bobby Jones outdrove me, but frustrated with myself nonetheless. *I can't hit this shot*, I thought, addressing the ball quickly, just wanting to get the failure over with. Holding the club lightly, I swung as hard as I could and actually caught it pure. Widening my eyes, I followed the shot as it barely trickled onto the front of the green some thirty feet from the pin. *Needed more club, but at least I got it on*, I thought, smiling and handing the club back to the caddy.

"You know, Johnnie, I'm probably going to need a little more stick," Bob said.

"Eight or seven?"

I watched as he picked a couple of blades of grass from the fairway and flung them into the air. The flecks drifted behind him to the right. "There's a little wind in our face." He paused, still gazing intently at the flagstick some one hundred forty yards away. "Let's go with the seven."

He took the club from Johnnie, continuing to peer at the green ahead. Finally, he addressed the ball and swung. His back swing was shorter, and he played the ball a bit farther back in his stance. The result was a low, penetrating shot that landed ten feet in front of the flag and bounced forward, cozying up to about three feet from the hole.

"Incredible," I said.

"Not really," Bob said. As we followed Johnnie toward the green, he asked, "You knew you couldn't get there with a nine iron, Randy. Why'd you hit it?"

I felt my face turning hot again, but I didn't want to play games. "You know why."

"Because I told Johnnie I was going to hit nine?"

I nodded. "Yes. I wanted to hit the same club that the great Bobby Jones was hitting. I didn't want to have to take more club."

"And yet I ended up changing my mind and hitting a seven iron, which was *two* clubs stronger than the nine."

"Nice trick," I said. "You do that in tournaments to folks? Play with their ego?"

"Actually, not much," he said. Then he smiled. "Well, maybe a few times, but this particular time I admit that I was testing you. One hundred forty yards slightly uphill and into the wind is gonna require the club you would typically hit one hundred fifty, maybe even one hundred fifty-five yards. I figured I'd have to hit at least an eight iron, but I wanted to see what you would do. So I told Johnnie to hand me the nine."

"And I fell right into the trap." As we reached the front of the green, I marked my ball with a coin that was in my pocket. I didn't remember putting the quarter in my pocket, but voilà. There it was. Just like the clothes I was wearing and my clubs being in the back of my trunk.

Not responding to my comment, Bob marked his ball.

While Johnnie tended the pin, I promptly putted my ball ten feet past the hole. As Bob was no more than three feet away from the cup, I was still out. Feeling frustrated and embarrassed, I re-marked my ball, glanced at the hole for a second, and hit the putt. This time, I came up a few inches short. Sighing, I tapped in for my bogey. As I was picking the ball out of the cup, Bob said, "When you screw up, get off the field, or the green in this case, as quickly as possible."

"You sound like my father."

"Smart man," Bob said. "Though I'm not sure that advice holds as true on a golf course as on a baseball or a football field." He paused as he walked to the side of the ball and took his stance. "In golf, after you've blasted a lag putt way past the hole, you still have a second putt." He looked up and peered at me.

I waited for him to add more, but he didn't. Instead, he addressed the ball and made a smooth stroke with his putter. I watched his ball, knowing that it would find the bottom of the cup, but a funny thing happened. The ball didn't go in. It caught the side of the hole and lipped out.

Behind me, I heard Johnnie whistle between his teeth.

Bob looked at me again without a trace of emotion on his face.

"You were robbed," I managed. "It was a good putt."

He nodded. "It was. I hit it exactly the way I wanted." Then he smiled. "And it didn't go in." He walked over to his ball and tapped it into the hole. He'd made a par four to my bogey five.

Bob handed his putter back to Johnnie as we walked off the green, and I did the same. As we approached the next tee box—the second hole, as I recollected, was a par three—Bob stopped by a tree and leaned his arm against it. Not looking at me, he spoke in his deep southern drawl. "I have a bad temper, did you know that, Randy?"

In the far reaches of my brain, I seemed to remember reading a biography of Bobby Jones that mentioned the fiery tantrums he'd thrown as a boy and a young man. "I think I've heard that before."

He gazed down at his golf shoes. "You ever throw your club in anger after hitting a bad shot?"

I smiled. "Many times. Always throw it in front of you, right? That way, you pick it up on your way to the hole instead of having to backtrack."

"Right," he said, still peering at the ground. "Ever hit anyone with a club you were throwing?"

I shook my head.

"I did," Bob said. "I hit a terrible shot in the 1921 U.S. Amateur. I threw my club and hit a spectator in the leg." He sighed. "Lucky I didn't kill the poor woman."

"Good grief." It was the only thing I could think to say, and it sounded stupid and dull coming out of my mouth.

"Got a letter from the USGA saying I needed to clean up my act."

"Well, I'd say you cleaned up pretty well. You won five U.S. Amateurs after that, didn't you?"

Finally, he looked up at me, his eyes radiating intensity. "I wouldn't have won anything if I hadn't learned to control my temper." He took a step toward me. I had always envisioned the great Bobby Jones as a tall man, but now, looking him right in the eye, I noticed that at six feet tall, I was actually several inches taller than the great champion. Still, as he leaned closer to me, I felt myself shrinking in his presence. "Being able to control yourself—your emotions, your temper, your ego, your thoughts, your imagination, your anxiety—has a tremendous impact on performance and success."

I couldn't help but smirk at him. "So does talent. You were a prodigy. You could break par by the time you were ten years old and were playing in national tournaments at fourteen, right? Self-control, my butt. What has the most impact on success and performance is God-given talent." I spat on the grass. "Look, I have no interest in living out a self-help book where dead ghosts spout on about things that everyone knows is true. Control your emotions. Work hard. Don't quit." I ground my teeth together. "That all sounds good until life grabs you by the throat and starts to squeeze."

Not waiting for his response, I turned my back on him and strode toward the second tee box. I bit my lip to stop it from quivering and gazed up at the sky. "Darby, get me out of here," I said out loud, wanting nothing more than to be left alone.

12

"HOW FAR?" I BARKED AT JOHNNIE AS I REACHED THE SECOND tee box.

"Well, it's about 178 yards. The wind is coming from the—"

"Give me the five iron."

His eyes widened, but he didn't hesitate. "As you wish, Mr. Clark."

I snatched the club from him and stuck my ball and tee in the ground. Without taking a practice swing, I took my stance and swung as hard as I could. I caught it pure and watched as the ball started just left of the flag and drifted to the right, coming to rest a couple of feet right of the hole.

"Nice shot!" Johnnie roared.

But I was still too angry to get any satisfaction from the shot. I handed him the club without a word.

"You've always played your best golf a little mad, haven't you?" Bob said, teeing his ball. I didn't watch his shot, instead peering off at the Tudor clubhouse. *I want out of here, Darby. Right now. I'm tired of this charade and I want out.*

"Nice shot, Bob," Johnnie said.

"Thank you."

I walked toward the green without looking at either the caddy or Bobby Jones. *Why am I so mad?* I wondered.

"You think you are being patronized," Bob said.

I didn't look at him as I picked up my pace. "You can read my thoughts too?"

"You think that it's easy for someone like me to say these things, because everything worked out for me. I won the Grand Slam. I won thirteen major championships. I founded the Masters golf tournament." He paused. "Am I right?"

"So, what if you are?"

"Randy, I want to show you something, come here."

"I'm gonna make my birdie and move on to the next hole, got it? You are one of my heroes, Mr. Jones, and under other circumstances, I might think this little dream was pretty cool, but—"

"But you're planning to kill yourself, and you don't have time to learn anything before you jump?"

I stopped and wheeled toward him. Legend or no, Bobby Jones was about to get his butt whipped. But when I turned, I noticed that he was holding his putter out in front of him with both hands. The grip end was closest to me.

"I want you to use this on your putt."

I blinked at him and then at the club he was holding. *Calamity Jane,* I thought. I was gazing at the most famous putter in the history of golf. I took hold of the club's grip with both hands and took a practice stroke. The club's rusty-bladed head looked irregular and small. *How in the world did he make all those putts with this thing?*

"You'll see," Bob said, gesturing toward the hole.

"But I'm closer to the hole than you. It's your turn."

"Go on. We can take some liberties with etiquette. We are the only players on the course."

I marked my ball and flipped it to Johnnie, who cleaned it with a towel and tossed it back to me. I placed the ball over the quarter and put the money back in my pocket. Then, as the caddy removed the pin, I addressed the ball. The worn leather grip felt soft in my hand, and I held the club lighter than usual. After looking at my line—the putt was almost dead straight—I made as smooth a stroke as I could muster. The ball dropped dead in the hole, and I couldn't help but smile.

"That putter has eyes, Randy, I would swear it," Bob said.

"Nice birdie, Mr. Clark," Johnnie chimed in.

I reached inside the hole to grab the ball but felt a strong tug on my fingers, and the next thing I knew I was hurtling downward into the ground. *What the . . .*

Seconds later, I was standing on a tee box surrounded by hundreds of people. There were men and women in the crowd, and I squinted to get my bearings. The men were wearing suits and ties, and the women had on light-colored dresses and hats. A golfer was approaching a teed-up ball, and I immediately recognized Bobby Jones. He appeared to be wearing the same thing he had on a few seconds ago, but we were no longer at East Lake. "Bob?" I whispered, but he ignored me. "Johnnie?" But I saw no trace of the Scottish caddy.

Before I could say anything else, I watched Bob hit his ball. On contact, I saw his face twist into a grimace. Then, after yelling something I couldn't make out, he hurled his club into the air.

Subconsciously, I brought my hands to the sides of my face, watching as the club seemed to twirl in slow motion down the left side of the fairway. Then I heard the squeal of a woman and a collective gasp from the audience. As Bob took off toward the sound of the scream, I heard several murmurs from the crowd. "Can you believe he did that?" a woman asked. "Come on, Bobby, you are better than that!" came a high-pitched male voice. "Spoiled little rich kid," a male baritone grumbled. "They should never let him play this tournament again."

I followed Bob down the fairway until he reached the spectator who had been struck by the club. This man, who a few moments ago at East Lake had looked unflappable, now was red-faced, his embarrassment and shame palpable. "Ma'am, I'm very sorry."

The woman, who was holding her knee with both hands and sitting on the grass, glanced up at him. "It's . . . okay," she managed.

Bob started to say something else, but then he sighed and began to walk away toward his ball. "They ought to kick him out of golf altogether," a voice rang out. I ran to catch up with Bob, who was walking with his head down and his hands stuffed deep in his pockets. Eventually, he looked at me with sad, defeated eyes. "Can I have my putter back?"

I glanced at my right hand and realized I was still holding on to Calamity Jane. "Of course." I handed the club to him. When he took it, he latched onto my left arm.

"Hey!"

The next thing I knew I was hurtling upward again. I closed my eyes as dizziness began to set in. When I opened them, I was back on the second green at East Lake and looking straight into the eyes of Bobby Jones. "How would you describe how I looked a second ago walking down the fairway after hitting that woman with my club?"

My legs felt shaky. "I don't know. Bad."

He squeezed my arm tighter. "Come on, Randy. Don't be lazy. Think about what you saw. What did I look like?"

I thought back to a few seconds ago. In all of the images I'd ever seen of Bobby Jones, he was the picture of confidence. Clear eyes and a charming smile on his face. His swing was always one of fluidity and grace, and everything about him oozed southern style. But the man who threw the club was none of those things. His swing had been faster and jerkier. And, after the incident, he had looked. . . . what? His hands had been in his pockets, eyes downcast.

"Think, Randy," Bob whispered.

"Defeated," I said. "Like a loser."

Finally, he let go of my arm. "Exactly."

I waited for him to say more, but he walked away, handing Calamity Jane back to Johnnie. I placed my hands on my knees and gazed down at the green grass. The world was still spinning from the vision Bob had shown me.

"Let's go, Randy," Bob called from ahead of me. "We have a lot more golf to play."

I took in a deep breath and rose up. When I did, I noticed that Johnnie was a foot away, gazing up at me with a mischievous grin on his face. "You look a bit pale, Mr. Clark." He reached into his pocket and pulled out a flask. "A little pinch of Scotch whiskey for you?"

I exhaled, thought about it for a second, and grabbed the container. I took a short pull and closed my eyes as the warm liquid eased down my throat.

"Better, aye?" Johnnie asked.

"Thank you," I managed, forcing myself to follow after him. I felt a bit steadier on my feet but still out of sorts.

"You know what hole Mr. Jones was playing when that club-throwing incident happened?" Johnnie asked.

I shook my head. "No."

"Hole number eleven . . . in the third round."

I waited for the punch line or point to whatever Johnnie was trying to say, but he said nothing.

"There was a lot more golf to play," Bob said from up on the tee box. "Twenty-five holes, to be exact. But I was already beaten." He paused. "I beat myself." He smiled down at me. "That ever happen to you?"

My eyes narrowed, thinking of all the times I'd lost control of my emotions in my short-lived golfing career. "You already know the answer to that, but I'll humor you. Sixteenth hole of Q school. Sharp dogleg-left par four. I hit a great drive and cut the corner. Had ninety yards to the flag. There was a sucker pin in the back-left portion of the green. Smart play is middle of the green. I went for the pin with a sand wedge and airmailed everything. Short-sided myself with a brutal chip, which I ran well past the flag and was so pissed about it that I three-putted. Double bogey."

"And you missed getting your card by one stroke, right?"

I nodded. "If I had collected myself after the bad shot from the fairway, I could've easily made a bogey. Might have even gutted out a par." I paused. "But I was so mad about the poor decision that—"

"—that the bad choice cost you two shots instead of one," Bob interrupted, and took another drag off his cigarette. "That's a good example. I'm sure that one keeps you up at night."

"Missed my chance at the tour," I said. "I could have been a professional golfer and lived my dream."

"You understand, don't you, Randy, that Q school I believe had six different rounds and one hundred eight holes of golf?"

"Is this where the wise guru and winner of thirteen majors tells me that one hole doesn't make a tournament and it wasn't that one lapse in control that cost me?" I stepped up onto the tee box. "I'm getting tired of all the patronizing, Bob. Can we just get on with it?"

He shrugged. "Didn't you birdie four holes in a row on the front side of that round?"

I looked at him, more curious now than angry. "What?" I finally asked.

"You birdied four holes in a row during that round. On the front nine. Four, five, six, and seven." He paused. "Remember how the eighth hole went?"

I tried to but couldn't. Everything about my failure at Q school had been whittled into the tunnel of what had happened on sixteen.

"Come on, Randy. Think harder. For someone so obsessed with a failure, I can't imagine you forgetting what happened on the eighth hole." Bob took another pull off his cigarette. Then, smiling, he reached into his pocket and flipped a ball toward me.

13

I TRIED TO CATCH THE BALL AS IT SPUN TOWARD ME, BUT BOB hadn't tossed it hard enough. The ball dropped in front of me. As I bent to pick it up, I saw that it was now on a tee. I pulled my hand back and stood up. Bob was no longer there. Neither was Johnnie. The tall pines and grandeur of the Tudor-style East Lake clubhouse behind us were gone, replaced by palm trees covering the sides of the fairway. The air, which I hadn't noticed before, was now sticky and sweltering. I felt sweat beads on my forehead. I glanced to my right and noticed a vaguely familiar face. The man was young, probably in his twenties, with a portly belly. His thin blond hair was covered with a white cap that said *Wilson Staff* in red letters on the top. He grinned at me, but his eyes weren't friendly.

"Damn, Clark. Four in a row. Have you thought about the tournaments you're going to play on tour next year?" His grin widened.

"Still got eleven holes left," I heard myself say, feeling my stomach twist into knots and knowing that this was the real me. I remembered now.

"The hard part of this dirt track is over," he said, and now I remembered his name. Dewey Barnett. He'd played the tour for a couple of years and lost his card. He'd regained his form and was well ahead of me by this point in the qualifying. He was all but in, but he knew I was on the bubble. He was a loudmouth who liked to stick around after rounds and wax poetic about his two years playing on the tour and the round he'd played with Arnold Palmer. I hadn't liked him much, and I remembered being frustrated that there were so many good golfers who seemed to share Dewey's attributes. Slightly overweight, drank too much, and certainly no rocket scientist or brain surgeon. *But the bastard made everything on the greens. If he was ten feet from the hole, the ball was going in.*

"And this hole is a piece of cake," Dewey added.

I looked down the fairway and agreed. A straight three-hundred-fifty-yard par four with a fairway as wide as an apartment complex. The only trouble was some trees that lined the left side. Still, I felt my arms tense. I also felt Dewey's piercing eyes on me.

I snatched the club back too quick during my backswing. I felt it immediately. Then, as the downswing began, I felt my hands moving in front of me, beginning to roll over too soon. I tried to hold up, but it was no use. When I made contact with the ball, it soared into the air and took an immediate left turn. The ball went deep into the trees on the left, and that was when I saw the white out-of-bounds stakes.

"Snapper," I heard Dewey say to the left of me. I glanced at him, and the grin had lessened a little but not much.

I had hit the dreaded snap hook, sometimes called a duck hook. It was literally the only shot I could possibly have hit that would have gotten me in trouble. I could have missed the fairway by one hundred yards to the right and still been in play.

"Tough break, Clark," Dewey said, but there was no empathy in his voice. I thought now of all the men I had played with over the years—in high school and college and on the mini tours—who loved nothing better than to needle you. That was part of the game, and the men on the Twickenham Country Club Big Team were professionals at it. Yet I still acutely felt the embarrassment and shame that I had endured those many years ago. I stuck my tee in the ground and placed my ball on it. I rose up and glanced at Dewey Barnett, bracing for his shark-like grin, but he was gone, and Johnnie was back. So was Bobby Jones. I could smell the scent of cigarettes.

"Remember it now?" Bob asked.

"Yes," I said.

"What happened next?" Bob asked, speaking in the tone of a high school teacher who already knows the answer.

"Re-teed and blistered one down the fairway. Hit a wedge to about ten feet and two-putted for double bogey." I shrugged. "Could've been worse. After the penalty stroke, I played the hole in par."

"Could've," Bob agreed. "Would it surprise you to know that only three players bogeyed that hole during all six rounds and that you were the only player in the field who carded a double bogey?"

I gazed down at the ball. "That sounds like something my dad probably said after the round. 'Randy, how in the world did you manage to double-bogey the easiest hole on the course?'"

"Well . . . how did you?" Bob asked, and there was the slightest tease in his voice.

I looked up at him. "Because I let Dewey get to me. I've always let the needlers get to me."

He stepped closer to me. "I agree, but it goes deeper than

that. You couldn't handle success." He gave me a kind smile. Unlike Dewey Barnett, Bob's eyes did hold compassion. "Self-control is more than controlling your temper when things go bad. It's managing your ego and your anxiety when things go good."

"How do you do that?"

He shrugged. "There is no easy answer to that question." His voice rose louder. "The bottom line, though, is that people who can control their emotions and anxiety, whether good or bad, happy or sad, have a better chance of success." He paused and licked his lips. "Otherwise, you're unstable. A tree with no roots. The least little change in emotional status acts like a gust of wind that knocks you off where you are trying to go." He took a final drag on his cigarette and tossed it to the ground, stomping on it with his shoe. "Randy, I spent seven years letting my emotions knock me out of the winner's circle. I was trying to beat the other players, but the only person I ended up beating was me."

"How did you overcome that?" He had me now. I was leaning toward him, eager to hear whatever the secret was. "How did you stop beating yourself?"

"I hit rock bottom."

I cocked my head at him. "What does that mean?"

But Bob had stopped looking at me and was now gazing down the fairway. The third hole at East Lake is a long and treacherous par four. "Birdie man is up," he finally said, nodding at me to go ahead.

14

THE NEXT FIFTEEN HOLES WERE A BLUR. I FELT LIKE OUR walks down the fairway and up to the green were accelerated. I knew I should probably try to enjoy the moment or "smell the roses," as my mother liked to say, but it was no use.

The eighteenth hole at East Lake is a two-hundred-yard par three that goes slightly uphill and is framed with the backdrop of the historic clubhouse to the left. I asked Johnnie for a three iron and watched as Bob teed his ball. I hadn't thought much about my score during this round, but I believed I was even for the day. If I had to guess, Bob was around three or four under. The question that I had held under my breath since our conversation after my flashback to Q school finally came out as he was sizing up his shot. "So, we're almost done here, Bob," I said, kind of half chuckling in an attempt to make light of things. "Are you going tell me what rock bottom was for you?"

He looked at me and then back up at the green. Ignoring my question, he approached his ball and, after taking his stance, hit a towering shot. I watched as the ball landed about fifteen feet to the right of the flag and came to rest even closer.

"Nice shot," I said.

"Thank you," Bob said, gazing up at the green and then letting out a long breath. "Rock bottom for me was 1921," he said, gazing down at the grass.

"The U.S. Amateur? Where you hit that lady?"

He shook his head. "That was the appetizer. The main course was at St. Andrews in the Open Championship."

"What happened?"

He peered up at me and smiled. "Come see for yourself."

I hesitated, wondering how it would happen this time. Bob's smile widened, and he gestured with his index finger for me to approach him. "Nothing dramatic this time," he said.

When I was next to him, he put his arm around me and pointed at the ground. "Look down for a few seconds."

I did as I was told.

"Now look up."

When I raised my eyes, my breath caught in my throat. Gone were the Tudor clubhouse of East Lake and the trees and undulating green fairways.

I was standing in the middle of a vast barren landscape. The ground was hard-packed brown sod that resembled dirt more than grass. And I didn't see a tree in sight. Instead, in the distance, I saw the grayish-blue water of the North Sea.

"St. Andrews," I whispered.

"Aye," Johnnie said, and I jerked my head toward him. The Scotsman was standing beside me. He hadn't been along for the ride on the past two flashbacks, but he was for this one. "What are—"

"There," he interrupted, pointing behind me.

I turned and saw young Bobby Jones striding toward us. His eyes were blank, and his face was pale. Sweat stood out on his forehead. When he stopped, I realized that we were standing on a tee box. I glanced to my right and saw a man holding a marker that read *Hole 11*. "That a six on the last hole?" Bob's partner asked, a golfer whom I did not recognize.

"Yes," Bob said, and the irritation in his voice was palpable. As Bob's playing companion wrote down the score, Johnnie pointed for me to look at the card. I stepped forward and my breath caught in my throat when I saw all the high numbers. "He's playing awful," I said.

"Aye," Johnnie agreed.

I peered at Bob, who was now gazing down at the barren sod of the Old Course. He didn't watch as his playing partner hit his drive. As Bob placed his tee in the ground, his demeanor was even worse than what I'd seen at the U.S. Open. Not only did he appear defeated, it was almost as if he didn't care anymore. He took his swing and the ball headed right. The groans in the crowd told the story. I saw Bob snatch his tee out of the ground and hand his club to his caddy without looking. Johnnie and I followed after them, as did the hundreds of spectators who lined both sides of the fairway.

Bob stopped at his ball in a thicket of weeds. Seconds later, he took a mighty swing, but the ball stayed put. Bob took another hack at the ball. This time, it came out of the brush but only a few yards and then disappeared again into the weeds.

"Good grief," I said, looking around and seeing the spectators' eyes all zone in on Bob. Many of them were shaking their heads. There were mostly frowns, but also a few smiles. The smiles weren't malicious, but rather the expression of someone who had also been bitten by St. Andrews's teeth. I watched Bob swing his club in frustration at where his ball had just been, sending another clod of weeds into the air. He cursed, and his shoulders sagged. He trudged forward to where the ball had come to rest and then looked across the fairway. I followed his line of sight and saw his playing partner standing next to his own ball with his hands on his hips, clearly waiting for Bob to hit again. Bob had swung twice and not advanced the ball past his partner. He was still "out" and would have to hit again.

Bob took his grip and aligned his feet. Seemingly without even looking at the hole, he swung and finally hit the ball flush. It arced in a right-to-left curve toward the hole and found the front of the green. Bob handed the club back to his caddy without a word of acknowledgment.

He's done, I thought. *He's beaten himself again.*

After Jones's partner hit his shot onto the green, Bob took a cursory glance at his ball and hit his putt several feet past the hole. Telling his partner he'd finish, he walked briskly up to the ball. *Get off the field*. I heard my father's admonition again in my mind, and I could tell Bob was thinking the same thing. Glancing at the hole, Bob lined up his body and putted. He followed behind the ball, clearly expecting it to go in. But instead of falling in the hole, the ball caught the lip and rimmed out. Bob stared at the ball like it had betrayed him in some way. Then, instead of knocking the ball in the cup, he leaned over and . . .

"No," I said out loud, but my words were of little use. I stood powerless as the great Bobby Jones picked his ball up. He walked toward his playing partner and extended his hand. The other man hesitated a moment but finally grasped Bob's hand. The look on his face was one of shock and disappointment. As I looked around the green and down the fairway at the spectators, I saw the same expression on most of their faces. Many of them had also become red-faced with anger.

"He's quit," a man said. "Bobby has quit."

Picking up his ball before the hole had been completed

served as an automatic disqualification. Bobby Jones had indeed quit. I ran toward Bob as he walked in the opposite direction of the hole. "You can't do that," I screamed at him. "These people came to see you play. You're Bobby Jones, for Christ's sake." But Bob continued to walk, his pace even brisker. When we entered the clubhouse, I expected to see the pro shop or a nineteenth hole, but instead we weren't at St. Andrews anymore.

We were now in a small room. There was a bed in the middle of it, and I thought of the scene I had witnessed with Darby Hays in the hotel room in Florida the day my son was buried.

This scene was different. There was no woman in the room. Bob sat on the bed in the otherwise spare room with his face in his hands. He appeared to be crying. When he finally lifted his head and his hands dropped away, I could see another emotion in the man's sunken eyes.

Shame.

"When you quit, regardless of whether it's a game or your life, it marks the ultimate loss of self-control." I turned and saw the shadow of Bob in the corner of the room. He had lit another cigarette and his face was illuminated for a moment by the glow of the match's ignition. "This was rock bottom for me," he said. "My family and friends were ashamed of me, and the sportswriters crucified me." He took a drag off the cigarette and cleared his throat. "I quit, and I had to deal with the shame of it wherever I went for the rest of my life."

"But you won," I said. "You won soon after this, didn't you?"

"I won the 1923 U.S. Open. That was over two years later."

I took a step closer to him and thought of the looks on the people's faces that I had just seen. The anger and outrage. I couldn't think of anything worse for a golfer to do than pick up his ball during a round and quit.

"There isn't anything worse," Bob said, again reading my thoughts.

"How could you recover from that? How *did* you recover?"

He took a drag off his cigarette and then pulled back the curtains on the window in the room. "Look."

I peered out the window and into the darkness, seeing nothing. "What am I looking for?"

"Watch," Bob said.

I kept my eyes on the glass in front of me. For a full minute, the scenery didn't change. Then, ever so faintly, I noticed a light in the distance. It started low in the east and slowly began to rise.

I glared at Bob. "You're doing it again."

"What?"

"Patronizing me with clichés. What is this one? Even as bad as things were, the sun still came up. Is that the lesson? Did you jump off this bed, throw open the window, and know that you were going to win thirteen majors? Maybe you saw a young man carrying a duck and asked him to cook it for the playing partner and fans you bailed on the day before? Old Ebenezer learns his lesson when he sees the sun?" I didn't wait for an answer. Instead, I headed toward the door. But when I tried to open it, I found it locked. I turned around and pointed at Bob. "I want out of here. I'm tired of this mess."

But the ghost in the corner was gone. Instead, the only person I saw in the room was the Bob Jones still lying in the bed. He was gazing out the window with sad eyes. "They'll never let me live it down," I heard him whisper.

Then, from behind me, I heard another match flicker. I turned back to the door, and the ghost of Jones was standing in front of it.

"The sun came up and I was just as depressed as before, but the cliché, as you call it, still holds true. The sun *did* come up. It came up each day for the next twenty-four and a half months. I went home. I took the criticism on the chin, but I kept playing. I may have quit at St. Andrews, but I didn't quit the game. I didn't quit on life."

"What did you do?"

"I kept trying. I knew that I had to control my temper and my emotions if I was ever going to win, and I eventually did."

"How?"

Bob smiled. "Part of it was maturity. I'm only twenty years old over there. I'd played a lot of golf but hadn't lived enough life." He paused and walked around me to the window. "You know that joke you just made about Scrooge calling for the boy with the duck?"

"Yes."

"Come here," he said, continuing to gaze out the window.

I sighed but did as he asked.

"Look," he said, pointing down to the street. "What do you see?"

I shrugged. "People."

"People doing what?"

"Come on, Bob, this is—"

"Answer the question." He cut me off and grabbed my upper arm.

I again lowered my eyes to the road below. "There is a couple walking with a kid in between them. An old man talking to another old man." I squinted. "Looks like a store owner is sweeping the walk out in front of his business."

"And beyond the street below the hotel. Look over there." He pointed toward the historic St. Andrews Clubhouse. I saw golf bags being carried by caddies and what looked to be play-ers putting on the practice green.

"Players and caddies showing up for another round," I said. "So what?" I asked, ripping my arm out of his grasp.

"So what?" he repeated, smiling up at me. "So, life goes on, Randy. I quit this golf tournament yesterday, and I'm moping over there on the bed in my sorrows, but those peo-ple down there"—he pointed again—"haven't stopped living. They are going about their business just like they would have if I hadn't quit yesterday. The golf tournament . . . the Open Championship . . . will also go on, and a local fellow named Jock Hutchison, born right here in St. Andrews, will win it." He paused and put his strong hands on my shoulders. "The tournament went on. *Life* . . . did go on." He turned and gazed at the twenty-year-old version of himself, who was peering up at the ceiling with a blank stare. "But there I am. Lost in my own little world of despair and defeat." He chuckled. "I'm not sure when I decided that the world didn't revolve around me. At some point, though, I realized that no matter how bad quit-ting the tournament had been, it wasn't near as awful as I had thought." He stopped and pulled back from me, and there was a glint in his eye. "Things are rarely as bad . . . or as good . . . as they seem."

Now it was me who took a step forward, and I stuck my finger in the golfing legend's chest. "When my son, Graham, died . . . that *was* as bad as it seemed. You are wrong, Bob."

His gaze never left mine. "I know, Randy." His voice was lower now. "When I lost the use of my legs . . . that was as bad as it seemed. I know it doesn't compare to the loss of a child, but I spent the last two decades of my life in back pain and my final fifteen years in a wheelchair." He again paused, pulling the pack of cigarettes out of his pocket. He took one out and placed it in his mouth but didn't light it. "Do you know how that felt? For a man like me, who had been the greatest golfer in the world, to not be able to play the game I loved?" Bob struck a match and lit the cigarette. "To not even be able to walk?"

I shook my head but didn't say anything. My thoughts now were on my son, and I was back in the hospital room. I could hear the monotone drone of the flatline and could feel the shadow of my father in the corner. Mary Alice's screams reverberated in my temples.

Bob took a puff on his cigarette. "Randy, on the day that the doctors told me I'd never walk again, the sun still set in the west. People worked their jobs. Ball games were played, and men and women fell in and out of love." He narrowed his gaze. "The same things also happened when Graham died. Life still went on. And though a few things are indeed as bad as they seem, life will always go on. It doesn't stop for me or you or anyone else." He sighed. "It just keeps coming."

I blinked tears from my eyes. "Not for me," I said. "When this bizarre dream finally ends, life is not going to go on for me."

"Randy, I understand that you are in a rut right now—"

"A *rut*?" I spat the word. "My bankruptcy is imminent; my marriage is on the rocks and I'm worth more to my wife and daughter dead than alive." I ground my teeth together. "Graham is dead, and I couldn't do a damn thing to help him. My father is dead, and I never *ever* made him proud of me." I paused and turned to the window, but the people below were gone. As was the light.

All I saw now was darkness.

I want to die, I thought, closing my eyes. For several seconds, perhaps even a minute, the room went silent. I no longer could feel Bob's presence, nor could I smell the scent of nicotine. When I felt a breeze on my face, I opened my eyes. When I did, my stomach tightened, and I let out a gasp. I was standing on the edge of the Tennessee River Bridge. I still had on my golf spikes, and I didn't dare move, knowing that any misstep could cause me to lose my balance.

"I think you're wrong." I heard Bob's voice from behind me, but I didn't turn toward it. "I don't think that's what you want at all," he continued. "I think you're scared. Afraid that I might be right. That life does go on."

Despite my predicament, I felt anger burning inside me. Where did this ghost get off talking to me like that? I turned my head and when I did, my right foot slipped on the ledge. My spikes shot out from under me, and I landed hard on the ground. Then I began to slip off the ledge. At the last moment, my fingers found purchase, and I gazed up at Bob.

"You're fighting awful hard to stay on this bridge for someone planning to jump."

I opened my mouth to refute him, but before I could get the words out, I lost my grip and began to fall backward. As I hurtled toward the river below, the ghost of Bobby Jones was no longer visible. All I could see was the gray sky above as I braced for contact. I reached my hands out, for what I have no idea.

At the last moment, I flinched and closed my eyes.

15

MY EYES OPENED WITH A JOLT. WHERE WAS I? WAS I DEAD? I thought of Bobby Jones's last words to me. *You're fighting awful hard to stay on this bridge for someone planning to jump.* And then I'd lost my balance.

Slowly I took in my car. *What am I doing in my car?* I glanced out the front windshield and noticed that I was in the parking lot of the old Monrovia Golf Course. The clubhouse trailer was just as it had been when I pulled up . . . *when?* I grabbed the latch on the door and climbed out of the car. My legs felt rubbery as I tried to get my bearings. It wasn't quite dark, but there was very little light. *Have I been in this car the whole time?* I had pulled into the lot when? Nine o'clock? Nine thirty in the morning?

I glanced at my watch. Seven thirty. I leaned my backside against the car, taking note of my clothes. I was back in the coat and tie I had worn this morning. Gone were the golf shirt and slacks that I had magically changed into before entering the trailer and the enchanted world of East Lake and Bobby Jones. I moved my eyes around the empty parking lot. It was getting dark. I looked past the trailer to the flat fairways of the old Monrovia Golf Course, thinking of the round of golf I'd played and the lesson that Bobby Jones had tried to convey. *Four heroes . . . four rounds . . .*

I took in a deep breath and exhaled. "Self-control," I said out loud, as I watched the sun set. "You're going to have to do better than that, Darb," I whispered, plopping down into my car and shutting the door. For almost a minute, I sat behind the wheel, listening to the engine and going over the round with Jones and some of the flashbacks he'd shared with me.

I had to admit it was fascinating seeing the great Bobby Jones in such bad shape after throwing his club and when he quit at St. Andrews. It made me feel a little better that a champion like Jones had struggled with controlling himself.

But he recovered, I thought, putting the car in gear and easing out of the parking lot. Bobby Jones had won thirteen majors from 1923 to 1930. He had retired after winning all four major titles—the Grand Slam—in 1930. *He stopped beating himself . . .*

As I reached Highway 72, I pondered where I should go. I had started this trek in the morning with the intention of jumping off the Tennessee River Bridge. But now, after the round with Bobby Jones, I felt tired and unsure of myself. Plus, I almost felt like I had already jumped once today, given the way the dream with Jones had ended. *I don't want to do it in the dark*, I thought, turning left to go home.

"Tomorrow," I whispered. "I'll do it tomorrow."

16

AT EIGHT FIFTEEN P.M., I PULLED INTO MY DRIVEWAY. MARY Alice's station wagon was in its customary place in the carport, and I parked next to it. As I got out of the car, I noticed Davis's rust-colored Jeep, her pride and joy, parked on the curb. Over the past two years, she had mowed lawns and babysat kids in the neighborhood, scrounging together enough money to buy the vehicle when she turned sixteen. When I wasn't home yet, Davis always parked on the street.

I didn't know what I'd done to deserve such a hardworking, conscientious, and dependable kid. *I'm going to secure her future tomorrow.*

I entered my home and breathed in the scent of hamburger meat and onion rings. I walked to the kitchen and grabbed a beer out of the fridge, smiling at the sack of Burger King on the kitchen counter. Sometimes Davis had to have her fast-food fix after golf practice.

As I walked into the back den, I saw my daughter sitting in my leather chair. She got out of it without being asked, her eyes glued on the TV.

"Where's your mom?" I asked, sitting heavily in the chair and taking a long sip from the stubby Michelob Light bottle.

"In bed, I think," Davis said.

"Already?"

"She may be in the bathroom. She's sick. She was throwing up when I got home from practice."

"I better go check on her," I said, setting down the beer. Before I got up, I looked at my daughter. Sitting on the couch with her hair tied up in a ponytail, Davis bore a striking resemblance to a younger version of Mary Alice. I managed a tired smile. "How was practice?"

"Played nine holes with only irons. Shot two over."

"That's not bad."

She shrugged. "Not good, either."

"What's the word from Augusta?"

Davis shrugged. "Jack shot seventy-four. Sounds like he hit the ball well but didn't make any putts."

I snorted. "How could he? With that broom he's putting with. Who's winning?"

"Ken Green shot sixty-eight. I've never heard of him. Norman is two back and so are Kite and Watson."

I sighed. "Oh well."

"Jack's still got a chance, Dad," Davis said, but I waved her off as I walked out. *No way*, I thought.

I entered the bedroom, but Mary Alice wasn't in bed. I knocked on the closed bathroom door a couple of times. "Honey? Are you okay?" When she didn't answer, I peeked inside.

My wife was in a bathrobe on her knees with both arms around the toilet. Just as I opened my mouth to say something, she leaned over the opening and vomited.

I stepped into the room and placed my hand gently on the back of her neck, caressing the skin. "Honey?"

She wiped her mouth but didn't look at me. "I think I have food poisoning," she managed, as she coughed and heaved again.

"I'm sorry," I said, patting her back and wishing there were something I could say or do to make things better.

"Please go," she whimpered, pushing my hand off her back before leaning forward and vomiting again.

"Are you sure I can't—"

"Please, Randy!" she cried, and then covered her mouth with her hands, her upper body shaking. "Please," she repeated.

I stepped away from her, watching my wife grit her teeth against the next bout of nausea. The scene reminded me of all the times in the last three years that I'd seen Mary Alice crying on the couch or in the bed, and all I could do was stand there, unsure of how to reach her.

I can't help her, I thought. *With this . . . with the loss of Graham . . . with anything . . .*

I shut the door to the bathroom and leaned my forehead against it. "What did you eat?" I asked.

"My mother brought over some meat loaf for lunch."

"Ahh," I said, and smiled despite myself.

"Oh, shut up. Don't you dare say anything smart." She continued to talk, but her words were drowned out by the sound of the commode flushing. All I was able to hear was, ". . . you know she means well."

"Are you sure there's not anything I can do for you? Need some water?"

"No. I've just got to get this mess out of my system. I think Davis picked you something up from Burger King." She coughed. "Where have you been? Did work run late?"

"Yeah. Long day at the office."

"I'm sorry," she said, and I winced. Here was my wife, puking her guts out, and she was sorry about my hard day. A cloak of guilt enveloped me.

"A letter from the hospital came," she said. "I put it on the coffee table in the living room."

I closed my eyes. "Did you open it?"

Another cough followed by a few sniffles. "They said suit would be filed in two weeks if we haven't paid." Then she heaved again.

"Don't worry about it, okay, hon," I said, seeing an image of the Tennessee River Bridge pop into my mind again. "I have a plan."

"Okay," she managed.

I turned to go but heard her call out my name. "Randy."

"Yeah?"

I looked at the door and saw it creak open a few inches. Her pale face was barely visible through the crack. "There's no way I can go to Darby's funeral tomorrow. I'm sorry. Can you go?"

Without thinking, I nodded.

"Charlotte mentioned that there was a favor she was going to ask of you. I . . ." Her lip started to quiver. "I'm sorry to make you go by yourself, but—" She abruptly stopped talking and turned away. A second later, I heard the awful sound of her stomach heaving.

"Don't worry about Darby's funeral or Charlotte," I said, raising my voice so she could hear over the flushing toilet. "I'll take care of it."

Her only response was a few sniffles and spits and another heave. *Damn it, Bee Bee.* Even I called Mary Alice's mother by the pet name that Davis had given her, and the poor woman did mean well, but this wasn't the first time one of her attempts to "help" had gone awry. I shook my head and trudged back into the living room. When I caught sight of the letter lying on the coffee table, I paused for a second.

I have a plan, I thought. But as I remembered the crazy dream I'd been thrust into today and the funeral I'd be forced to attend tomorrow, I wondered if that was true anymore. Then, as I eased into one of the chairs at the kitchen table, I heard the ghost of Bobby Jones again in my ear. His voice was soft but firm. *You're fighting awful hard to stay on this bridge for someone planning to jump.*

SECOND ROUND

17

THE FUNERAL OF REGINALD DARBY HAYS TOOK PLACE AT NOON the following day at the Trinity United Methodist Church of Homewood, a suburb of Birmingham. I arrived fifteen minutes early and immediately noticed Charlotte at the front of the sanctuary. At thirty-four years old, Charlotte Hays was six years younger than me and a decade Darby's junior. She and Darby had met at a tour stop in Naples, Florida, about ten years earlier. "Randolph, Ms. Charlotte is the most striking woman I've ever laid eyes on," Darby had told me afterward, and he hadn't been lying. Even now, at the funeral of her husband and wearing a long black dress fit for mourning, Charlotte Hays stood out with her auburn hair, fair skin, and tall, athletic frame. I strode down the aisle, hoping to give her a hug before the ceremony began. When she caught my eyes, she stepped around a couple of people and fell into my arms. "Oh, Randy. He loved you so much."

"I'm sorry, Charlotte. Mary Alice would have been here,

but she is home with a terrible stomach bug." I paused. "I'm really going to miss him."

She nodded and bit her lip. "You know you were his best friend. He . . . really didn't have that many friends."

I snorted. "Darby was the pied piper, Charlotte. He never met a stranger. He had more friends than I could ever count."

Charlotte's hazel eyes glistened, and she shook her head. "No. He didn't."

Before I could respond, the preacher pulled her away. "We need to go over the final details, Mrs. Hays," he said.

Charlotte looked at me. "Find me afterward. I . . . hope you will do something for me. Please?"

"Of course," I said. "Anything."

THE CEREMONY WAS SHORT AND SWEET. THE LORD'S PRAYER was recited; Darby's niece sang "Amazing Grace"; the pastor said a few words of greeting to "celebrate the life of Reginald Darby Hays"; and, finally, Darby's younger brother, Cliff, did the eulogy, telling some old family stories and providing the general theme, also echoed by the minister, that Darby Hays was a man people looked up to and respected. A fun-loving man who was always the life of the party. A man who would be sorely missed by his family and friends.

I thought Darby would have been proud of his brother's speech and the turnout. There must have been two hundred people in the church. As the ceremony ended with the singing of "Jesus Loves Me," which Cliff said was his brother's favorite hymn, I couldn't help but think of the ghost of Darby Hays that I had seen in my dream two nights earlier. Of sitting in my friend's ruined Jaguar. Of hearing how little he had thought of his own life.

I wasn't going to burden Charlotte with any of it, if indeed Darby's ghost had told me the truth.

I don't know what's real and what's not anymore, I thought, wondering what I had done all day yesterday while I was supposedly playing golf with Bobby Jones and a Scottish caddy named Johnnie. Had I been parked in front of the old Monrovia clubhouse trailer the whole time? Had I really been transported to East Lake and to St. Andrews yesterday?

Am I losing my mind?

It was a fair question. I was seeing visions of dead people. I was blacking out for long periods of time. And, before and during these hallucinations, I was contemplating suicide.

Perhaps it was more than just a fair inquiry. *It's an easy one. I am losing it, there's no other explanation. I've decided to kill myself, and my body and soul are in self-preservation mode. They have jumbled my mind to keep me from going through with it.*

As I hummed the closing hymn, I tried to shake off the thoughts. I was grateful that Charlotte would give me a task to occupy my time.

I peered toward the coffin at the front of the church, and my thoughts drifted to the last funeral I had attended. Dad's service was held graveside with only family and close friends in attendance. I had sat next to my mother, whose demeanor remained stoic throughout the brief sermon and at the reception at my house afterward. She had never let any of us see her cry, thinking, as always, of other people's feelings instead of her own. Only when I drove her home that night had she finally released a few long-suppressed sobs.

I hadn't cried at my father's death or his funeral. The cancer had slowly eaten up his pancreas over the course of nine months and moved into his bones. By the end, he'd lost eighty pounds and was almost unrecognizable as the roughneck bricklayer he'd been during his working life. By then, even Mom, if she'd been given a truth serum, would have said she was relieved when he passed on.

Did I love my father?

I took in a deep breath and rubbed my eyes. The answer was yes. I worshipped him.

Did he love me?

One of my fondest memories of Dad was watching the 1975 Masters together at my house, almost exactly eleven years ago. He had come over to help me finish installing a fence in the backyard, and we had caught the back nine together. There were no mushy moments. No "I love you, son" or "I'm so proud of you, Randy." We had merely sat on the couch in my living room and watched Jack Nicklaus win his fifth and likely final Masters title together. We were both rooting for Jack, me probably harder than Dad. We had made small talk about the swings of the different players, the beauty of the course, and, of course, Jack's forty-foot snake of a putt on the sixteenth hole, which won him the championship. We had both risen to our feet to watch that putt. When it went in, I remembered screaming "Yes!" at the top of my lungs. I turned to my father, who had a wide smile on his face. He hadn't said anything, but he had pumped his fist once.

I bowed my head as the preacher gave the benediction and again rubbed my eyes. When I did, I felt the wetness on my fingers and realized that I had shed a few tears. Most of my memories of Dad were a blur of instructions, admonitions, and orders. But in April 1975, we had shared an experience. It had only been a moment, but sometimes, I guess, maybe that's all we have in life. Moments . . .

Did he love me?

Yes, I thought. That was probably why I had so much resentment built up inside me. My father loved me, but his way of showing it left a lot to be desired. *Why couldn't he have supported me? A pat on the back after a bad round? Some encouraging words before a big tournament? Anything?* All I could remember was the criticism of my shortcomings. When Dad provided encouragement, there was always a hard lesson behind it. *Get up and work to support your family. Give up golf and turn to law because it is practical and responsible. Be strong for your family after Graham's passing because you're the head of the household and your wife and daughter will look to you to set the example.*

He wasn't a hugger and he didn't talk in flowery words. His world was black and white. Right was right. Wrong was wrong. And if you weren't good enough, you weren't good enough. It was that simple. And when the person who wasn't good enough happened to be his own son, he didn't sugarcoat the sad reality of life.

There comes a point in every man's life when he realizes that he's not going to be Joe Namath.

I gave my head a jerk and set my jaw, tired of my own thoughts. I opened my eyes and looked past the praying congregation to the closed casket directly behind the pastor. I thought about my deceased friend, whom I hadn't known as well as I thought.

Darby Hays was a frustrated and sad man.

Weak. I heard my father's rough voice in my head. Over the years, Dad's hard way of talking had become ingrained in my subconscious. I hated the thoughts it provided, but they were there nonetheless.

Darby was weak. If he'd had someone who kicked him in the butt a few times, then maybe he wouldn't have turned to drugs and other women.

I closed my eyes tight, hating myself for thinking in such harsh terms about my best friend.

Then hating my father and his harsh way. I loved the man. I hated the man.

I worshipped the man. And I was perpetually tormented by him, even from the grave.

AS EVERYONE FILED OUT OF THE CHURCH, I FOLLOWED SUIT. I waited under the shade of an oak tree for Charlotte. As I leaned my back against the thick trunk, my mind drifted back to the hotel room at St. Andrews and the blank, depressed eyes of Bobby Jones. *He recovered. He came back from picking his ball up and quitting a major championship. He came back and redeemed himself . . . and became a legend.*

I shook my head and gazed down at the roots that tunneled out from the tree. *He wasn't facing a two-hundred-fifty-thousand-dollar hospital bill. His son didn't die of cancer. He came back, but he wasn't as far gone as me.*

"Randy?"

I glanced up and saw Charlotte Hays standing in front me. She regarded me with red-rimmed eyes and touched my arm. "Are you okay?" she asked.

I wondered if I had blacked out again. I hadn't been taken anywhere else—no sudden flashbacks or anything—but by the worried expression on Charlotte's face, I must have looked out of sorts. "Yeah," I said. "Just . . . thinking about Darb." It wasn't necessarily a lie, but I still felt guilty for saying it. My guilt increased when I saw fresh tears forming in Charlotte's eyes. I pulled her in for an embrace, and for a few seconds, she cried into my shoulder.

"I'm sorry," she whispered. "I just can't believe he's gone, you know?" She squeezed my shoulders and I could feel her hands clenching into fists. "And I'm so *mad* at him. Drinking and driving. Throwing his life . . . and our whole future away."

She pulled back, holding my forearms tight with her fingers. "And everyone is wrong about him. Cliff, the pastor . . . everyone."

"What do you mean?"

"Darby may have acted happy-go-lucky and been a barrel of laughs around his friends and family, but . . ." She wrinkled her face and fought back more tears.

"But what, Charlotte?"

"He wasn't happy," she said, speaking now through clenched teeth. "He was miserable. He hated that he couldn't putt well enough to play the tour anymore, and he was filled with regrets for not winning more tournaments and being a better player." She let go of my arms and wiped her nose. I reached into my suit jacket pocket and pulled out a handkerchief, which she took without asking. She blew her nose and looked up at the sky. "He wanted other things too . . . but we couldn't . . ." She trailed off. "Here." She tried to give me the handkerchief, but I held up my palms in protest.

"Please. Keep it," I said, feeling a new rush of sorrow. Darby had never shared any of his problems with me.

She nodded and then, for a few moments, we both stared at the ground. I felt the wind on the back of my neck and realized for the first time that it was a pretty day. *A good day for golf*, I thought, and smiled, knowing that the pleasant weather was appropriate for my friend's burial and hoping he was getting a round in on that big country club in the sky. *Maybe with Bobby Jones and Johnnie . . .*

I felt Charlotte's hand grasp my own, and I looked at her.

"Can you do something for me, Randy?"

I gave her hand a squeeze. "Yes, what is it?"

She took a deep breath. "Darby spent a lot of time out at Shoal Creek. It was literally his favorite place in the world. He had a locker out there, and I think he kept some things there that were special to him. With everything that's happened since he died, I haven't been able to make it out to Shoal. Part of it is I don't want to have to drive the same road where Darby was killed . . ." She paused, and I could tell she was fighting hard not to cry again. She clasped her hands together to keep them from shaking. "I also don't think it should be me that cleans out his locker. Shoal Creek was . . . *sacred to him*. Golf, in so many ways, was Darby's church. He probably has some things in his locker that were very important to him, and I wouldn't understand the significance of them. Do you understand?"

I nodded.

She peered up at me. "I trust your judgment. If you think there is something I should see, then please bring it by the house. If you don't, then keep the item or throw it away. Whatever you want to do is fine with me."

"Are you sure?" I asked. "What about Cliff?"

"I thought about asking him, but I think it would be better if you did it." She sighed. "I'm also worried there may be some things in there that Darby wouldn't want me or his family to see."

"Like what?"

Her gaze narrowed to a glare. "Like his girlfriends' phone numbers. A pair of stray panties from a romp with one of the cart girls or one of his playing partners' wives."

The intensity of her eyes caused me to lower mine to the ground. "I see," I said.

"You knew my husband better than anyone. Am I wrong to suspect those things?"

Still gazing at the roots coming out of the bottom of the oak tree, I shook my head. "No," I said, realizing I should have been able to anticipate why Charlotte had levied this request. "I'm sorry," I added.

"Don't be, Randy. I loved that man. I knew he messed around with other women, but I loved him all the same. We were a good team, and let me tell you a little secret." She lowered her voice to a whisper. "Darby wasn't the only one who strayed."

My eyes darted up from the ground. I couldn't believe my ears.

She chuckled bitterly. "Oh, don't be such a prude. Darby and I had problems, and we dealt with them in our own ways." She paused. "Not everyone can have a marriage like you and Mary Alice, Randy."

I again cast my eyes downward and began to wish I could unhear what Charlotte had just shared. "Mary Alice and I aren't perfect," I managed, thinking about how distant my wife and I had become since Graham's death and the utter uselessness I felt at not being able to do anything to help us get over the loss of our son.

All I can do to help is jump.

"None of us are," Charlotte said. "But you guys come as close as you can. You give her a hug for me when you get home."

I again peered down at the ground, feeling guilt begin to saturate my being as I thought of my wife, whom I had last seen curled up in the fetal position in bed, still suffering from the effects of her mother's meat loaf.

"Will do," I whispered. Sucking in a short breath, I raised my eyes and leaned forward to kiss her cheek. "I should probably head to Shoal," I said, and she gave me a nod.

I started to walk away, but Charlotte's voice stopped me. "Randy?" There was a crack in the last syllable.

"Yeah," I said, turning back to her.

"Thank you for doing this."

18

I DROVE DOWN HIGHWAY 280 IN A BIT OF A HAZE, LOST IN thoughts of Darby, Charlotte, and the secrets in people's lives that take place behind closed doors. I thought that Darby was living the dream and the picture of success and happiness.

And I couldn't have been more wrong.

I remembered something that Bobby Jones had said in our round yesterday. *Things are rarely as bad . . . or as good . . . as they seem.* I knew that was true, but, on the flip side, I thought things had to at least resemble how they seemed.

Maybe not. I answered my thought as I turned on to Hugh Daniel Drive. Sucking in a deep breath, I slowed my vehicle as I began to navigate the curvy road. It was only dangerous if you were reckless with your speed, as Darby had been. I scanned each curve, trying to remember where his Jaguar had gone off the road, but the police had cleared the area and I found it impossible to distinguish one bend in the road from the next. When Hugh Daniel dead-ended, I took a left onto Highway 41. About a mile up on the right was the entrance to the club. I slowed when I reached the gate and rolled down my window. A uniformed guard stepped out of the security house adjacent to the gate and approached my car. "Can I help you?" he asked.

"I'm a friend of Darby Hays, a member who died in a car accident earlier this week. His wife asked that I go through his locker for her."

"Oh, yes. You are Mr. Clark. Mrs. Hays said you'd be dropping by. I'm so sorry about Mr. Darby. He was a really good man. Always very friendly with me and called me by name."

I glanced at the tag on the man's uniform, which read *Irvin*. "Thank you, Irvin," I said.

He nodded. "Please tell Mrs. Hays how sorry I am."

"Will do."

"I'll notify the pro shop you're on your way."

Before I could answer, Irvin turned and walked briskly back to the house, reaching his hand inside the door. A second later, the gate began to open. As my car wound down the path toward the clubhouse, I tried to remember the last time I was here. *Last summer? Or was it two summers ago?* Whenever it was, I had come up to play in a two-man scramble with Darby, and we had won the tournament. We had closed down the nineteenth hole afterward, celebrating the victory and wisely taking a taxi back to Darby's house. *Good times*, I thought, but I only half believed it. Were we really having a good time? Or were we both just escaping our lives for a few hours?

Either way, it had been the last time I'd seen my friend since his ghost appeared to me a couple nights earlier.

I parked at the bag drop and hopped out of my car. Before I could make it to the sidewalk that led down to the pro shop, a young attendant was trotting up the steps to meet me. "Mr. Clark?"

"Yes, hey."

"Follow me. I'll take you to Mr. Hays's locker."

When we reached the landing, I glanced to my right at the green expanse of golf course that lay before me. The Jack Nicklaus–designed course was a thing of beauty with its tree-lined undulating fairways and bent-grass greens. Shoal Creek had been one of Jack's first course designs, following Muirfield Village in Columbus, Ohio. Now, the Golden Bear had courses popping up everywhere, and it was obvious that golf course design would be his passion after his playing days were over. As I thought of Jack, my mind drifted to Augusta for a half a second. The second round was today, and Jack would probably need to shoot at least par to make the cut.

As we reached the mahogany door that led inside, I shook off the thoughts and tried to focus on the job at hand. I was nervous at what I might find in Darby's locker. *Please God, don't let there be a pair of panties in there . . .*

I followed the young attendant down a long hallway, which was decorated with portraits of famous courses and players, including Lee Trevino, who had won the PGA Championship here at Shoal Creek two years earlier. When we entered the locker room, we turned a corner, passing Jack Nicklaus's locker, which Darby always made a point to show me every time I had played with him here. Finally, a few rows over, the attendant stopped and pointed. "Here it is, sir." *Darby Hays* was stenciled in gold over the brown mahogany finish.

"Everyone loved Mr. Hays," the attendant said. "It was an honor to be able to talk and play with someone who had been on the tour." The boy paused. "I'm sure going to miss him."

"I know, son. Me too."

He handed me a box and a short, stubby key.

I thanked him as he trotted away. Then, sighing, I turned toward the locker.

19

I'D LIKE TO SAY THAT MY FRIEND'S LOCKER WAS A TREASURE chest of surprises and untold secrets. But, alas, that would not be true. There were two pairs of golf shoes in the bottom cubby, one all white and one white and black. In the large middle section, there were some khaki slacks and two golf shirts hanging on adjacent hooks. On the top shelf, I saw two folded sweaters, several caps, and a shaving kit.

In between the middle and bottom shelves of the locker were two drawers. I pulled open the one on the left and saw a stack of scorecards. Most of these were from Shoal Creek, but there were others from Birmingham Country Club, Atlanta Athletic Club, Pebble Beach, and several other famous courses. There was even one from Augusta. I opened that one and saw three names written on the card. Darby Hays, Jack Nicklaus, and Tom Watson. *I'll be damned*, I thought, looking over the scores. Darby had shot a sixty-eight, Jack had fired a seventy, and Watson a seventy-one. *That's a framer*, I thought, rubbing my thumb over the signatures at the bottom.

I also saw the card from Twickenham Country Club, where Darby had shot fifty-seven. He hadn't let me tell anyone at the club about his breaking the course record, but he had thought enough of the round to keep the card. I had to admit I was touched. I put the Twickenham card in my pocket.

I opened the second drawer and saw a small red spiral notebook. I wiped the dust off the unmarked cover and turned to the first page, dated seven years ago. *February 22, 1979.* Below it were a few sentences scribbled in my friend's handwriting. *Good practice round today at Riviera. Still haven't figured out how to play 18. Made some putts. Can I make them when it counts? Going out tonight.* Then *February 24, 1979.* Darby had written a shorter message. *Missed practice round yesterday because I was so hungover and had to take Sally home. Another tour groupie. When am I gonna grow up?*

For a moment, I felt bad reading my old friend's inner thoughts, but I knew that no one in his family, especially Charlotte, would want any part of this experience.

That's why she asked me to come.

Scanning the empty locker room, I noticed a sitting area with two leather chairs near the back. Sucking in a deep breath, I walked over and sat down. After only a brief hesitation, I continued to read the diary of Darby Hays.

THE FIRST PAGE WAS A HARBINGER OF THINGS TO COME. AT least ninety percent of the entries had some combination of frustration over putting, shame over cheating on Charlotte or drinking too much, and disappointment over a mediocre finish in a tournament. There were long gaps between entries and then flurries where every day for two or three weeks had a few sentences.

As I skimmed through it, I stopped on March 3, 1983. *Randy's son died today. Charlotte says we should go to the funeral, but I told her I can't withdraw from the tournament. She thinks I should at least call Randy, but I don't know what to say. The truth is that I'm jealous of my old friend. We've been trying to have a baby for six years. Randy's son may be dead, but at least he had a son. And he still has Davis. I know it is awful to feel these things, but I can't help it.*

Though I was angered by the callousness of my friend's words, I was more surprised than anything. *Darby was jealous of me?*

There was no entry at all on March 6, the day of Graham's funeral. I continued to skim until I came to April 11, 1984, more than a year later. *Another Masters in the books, probably my last. Gonna retire at the end of the year if I can't score any better. Was great to see Randy. So glad that he, Mary Alice, and Davis made it down. I know they are all still depressed over Graham's death, and I wish there were something I could do. As much as I love the guy, sometimes I think my presence makes things worse for Randy. It's sad. He would've given anything to be a PGA Tour pro, and I'd trade every dime I've made on the golf course to be a father. Ain't life grand?*

I reread the passage, and any irritation I'd felt toward my friend dissipated. Darby had never said anything to me about his desire to have children or the problems he and Charlotte were having conceiving a child. I thought back to what Charlotte had said at the funeral. *He wanted other things too . . . but we couldn't . . .*

I closed the binding and gazed around the empty locker room, feeling a sharp sense of sadness. My friend's journal reflected a life saturated with regret and loss, which he had kept hidden from me.

Finally, I stuck the diary under my arm and grabbed the

box. Then, sighing and taking a last look at Darby's locker, I headed back to the pro shop.

WHEN I REACHED THE DOOR, THE YOUNG ATTENDANT WHO had taken me to the locker room an hour earlier opened it for me.

"All done, Mr. Clark?"

"Yeah, son," I said. "Do you think you could have someone run this box out to Mrs. Hays's house?"

He smiled and nodded. "I'll do it myself, sir."

I was turning to leave, the diary in my hand, when the boy's voice stopped me.

"Mr. Clark?"

I looked back at him, trying not to appear impatient. I was so ready to get out of there. "Yeah?"

"There was a man who came in looking for you earlier . . . while you were going through Mr. Hays's things. He said he would wait out by the driving range."

"Did he say what he needed?"

The boy shook his head. "Only that you would want to talk with him."

I sighed. *What now?* "Did he leave a name?"

"Yeah," the boy said. "Ben."

I narrowed my gaze. "Ben? That's it?"

The kid nodded. "He said you would know him."

20

I THINK I KNEW WHO "BEN" WOULD BE EVEN BEFORE I WALKED out of the pro shop.

He said you would know him . . .

Off the top of my head, I couldn't think of a single "Ben" that I had been acquainted with in my life who would possibly want to talk with me on the Shoal Creek Golf Club driving range at three p.m. on a Friday. As I began to walk down the paved path to the driving range, the feeling of knowing the man waiting for me only intensified. *It's happening again*, I thought, as I felt the landscape to the side of me begin to shift and change. Before my eyes, the vast putting green in front of the clubhouse faded into a wide-open expanse. The men I had seen below the clubhouse, playing Shoal's signature fourteenth hole, also disappeared from view. I wheeled, and the brick façade of the clubhouse was gone too. For a moment, the world turned dark, and then, as if the sun had begun to rise much faster than normal, I saw freshly cut green grass in all directions. There were a few trees, but nothing like the scenery at

Shoal Creek. Turning 360 degrees, I felt like I was in a large green prairie. The many elevation changes that were present at Shoal Creek were gone. This ground was much flatter, though up ahead, where the driving range at Shoal had been a few seconds earlier, I saw a small hill. At the top of this crest was a tree.

In its shade a man was hitting golf balls alone.

"Sweet mother of God," I whispered. The man was slightly built. He couldn't be more than five feet, eight inches tall and around 140 or 150 pounds. He wore brown tailored slacks, black golf shoes, and a gray cardigan sweater over a white golf shirt.

On his head, he wore a white ivy cap. Some folks called it an ascot, a cabbie cap, or a duckbill cap. In my lifetime, I had simply called it the same thing my father had.

A Ben Hogan cap . . . The signature headpiece worn by one of the greatest golfers to ever live. My father had owned only one golf picture. It was of Ben Hogan, holding his follow-through, after hitting a one iron on the eighteenth hole at Merion. The shot had landed on the green and clinched a playoff spot for Hogan in the 1950 U.S. Open, which he would eventually win. Some called it the greatest pressure shot ever hit in competition.

As I approached closer, I felt my heartbeat racing. I looked behind me and saw part of a fairway and a tee box. In the distance, I saw the top of the flag of another hole. I was on a golf course, but it wasn't Shoal Creek Golf Club in Birmingham, Alabama. I turned back to the figure hitting balls under the tree. The first instructional book I'd ever read on golf was Hogan's *Five Lessons: The Modern Fundamentals of Golf.* And now here he was, the man himself, in living color. Or dreamlike color. *Whatever.* He had taken his stance and cocked his head toward a target in the distance. I followed his eyes, noticing the

intense concentration. His peers had given Hogan the nickname "Hawk," and it was easy to see why. He waggled the club,
again peering at the target. Then he swung, and I marveled at
seeing his signature flat backswing, the pronounced lateral slide
from his right leg to his left and the speed of his hips and hands
as he fired through the ball. The pace of his move was brisk, but
the confidence with which he brought the clubhead to impact
was palpable. When he struck the ball, it sounded like a cannon
going off, and I followed the arc of the shot until it landed about
one hundred fifty yards down the fairway. There was a chair
that he'd set there for a target, and from what I could tell, he'd
hit about fifty balls all within five feet of the chair.

As he held his follow-through, I took a step forward and
cleared my throat. "Mr. Hogan?"

He continued to look at where his ball had landed, and I felt
as if he hadn't heard me at all. He glanced down at his divot,
then back to the target. Finally, he set the club against the tree
and lit a cigarette. He blew a stream of smoke out of his mouth
and inspected me. When he did, I felt my stomach clinch. I had
been in awe of Bobby Jones, but being in the presence of Hogan was different. Jones had been friendly. Approachable. Even
amiable.

The man peering at me now with his Hawk-like gray eyes
beneath the brim of his cap was none of those things. There was
a coldness to the man's gaze.

"Why are you here?" he asked. His voice was firm, direct,
and even cooler than his glare.

I forced a chuckle. "I don't know. I—"

"Yes, you do," he snapped, taking a drag from his cigarette.
The coldness of his initial tone had been replaced with impa-
tience.

I licked my lips and decided to get right to it. "I was visited by the ghost of my dead friend, Darby Hays, a couple of nights ago. He said I'd be given a great gift. I'd get to play a round of golf with four of my heroes." I paused, noticing that Hogan's face remained utterly expressionless. "I believe that each hero has a lesson to share with me."

For a long moment, perhaps five seconds, Hogan said nothing, and his face remained stoic. Then, finally, he smirked. He dropped his cigarette and stomped it out. He rolled another ball over from the bucket that he'd dropped in front of the tree. He carefully nudged the ball to the front of a divot that must have been two feet long. *No telling how many balls he's hit to produce that long a divot*, I thought.

He glanced down the fairway at the chair, waggled the club, and launched another shot. This one clanged off the plastic seat. A perfect shot that might have gone in the hole if there had been a hole there.

"Great shot!" I said.

He held his follow-through and didn't acknowledge the compliment.

"What club are you hitting?" I asked, trying to break the ice.

Still without looking at me, he said, "Seven iron."

"You have a beautiful swing," I said, feeling lame as soon as the words left my mouth.

He smirked again. "No, I don't. What I have is a functional swing. The only beauty in it is that it works."

I smiled. "Some folks would call any swing that works beautiful."

He didn't smile, but his eyes creased a bit. Could the ice be thawing? "Perhaps," he admitted.

I took in a deep breath. "So, where are we?"

"Shady Oaks Country Club. Fort Worth, Texas."

The name rang a bell. "Is this where you grew up playing?"

"No. I learned how to play as a caddy at Glen Gardens, a little south of here."

I bit my lip, half wishing my father were here. He knew the Hogan backstory a lot better than I did, but now I remembered. Shady Oaks was the club that Hogan helped found in the late 1950s after the thrust of his playing career was over. "Why here?" I asked.

He pierced me with another glare. "Because I like it here."

I nodded and steeled my nerves. "So . . . are we going to play?"

"Tell me about your first round."

"Well . . . I . . ." I wasn't sure where to start. "It was the craziest thing. I pulled into the old Monrovia Golf Course and when I stepped inside, the place transf—"

"Just give me the lesson," he snapped. "What did you learn from your time with Mr. Jones?"

I cocked my head at Hogan's ghost, a bit taken aback by his calling one of his peers "Mr."

"Self-control," I finally said. "The point of . . . Mr. Jones's lesson was that I needed to learn how to control my emotions. My temper. My thoughts." I paused. "Everything."

Hogan said nothing. He rolled another ball over and, without any acknowledgment of me, he made his patented swing. The ball again landed square in the seat of the chair one hundred fifty yards away.

I shook my head in awe. "That's unbelievable," I said.

"What is?" he asked, his voice harsh, as he continued to hold his follow-through.

"You hit the chair twice in a row."

"That's my target, isn't it?"

"Yeah, but . . ." I trailed off, not wanting to upset the man . . . or ghost . . . any further. He seemed on edge, ready to pounce at any wrong word that might come out of my mouth.

"Mr. Jones was a great man," Hogan said, moving another ball to the front of his divot and gazing down at it. "And he's right. A person has to stop beating himself before he can win." He paused and took his stance. "And that starts with self-control." He swung and launched another shot into the afternoon air. This time, I wasn't even surprised when the ball clanged off the chair. "But that's not enough."

"What do you mean?"

Hogan set his club against the tree and lit another cigarette. After blowing a smoke cloud into the air, he scowled at me. Though I was getting used to the coldness of the man's gaze, the intensity behind his eyes still caused my stomach to tighten.

"Is self-control going to bring your boy back?"

I felt heat on my cheeks and behind my eyes.

"Is it?"

I swallowed, and, for a moment, I could smell the disinfectant from the hospital room. It was an hour after Graham's body had been moved out, and we were getting his things. Housekeeping had already been in, and the tile floors and bathroom reeked of the lemony scents of different cleansers. My boy was gone, and that room was going to be occupied by another patient. Some other poor wretch who would live or die based on the judgment of medical providers and the grace of God.

"No," I whispered.

"You can control your thoughts. You can have complete

mastery over your emotions." Hogan seemed to be talking more to himself than me, but I was now hanging on every word. "But your boy ain't coming back, Clark. He's dead."

Now I felt hot tears streaming down my cheeks, and my hands clenched into fists. *Who does this guy think he is?*

"You watched him die. You couldn't do one thing for him."

"I want you to shut up," I said, feeling my legs and arms beginning to shake with anger. I forced my feet to move and I approached the tree, glaring at the other man.

"And now you're going to kill yourself, aren't you?" Hogan's cold voice didn't scare me anymore.

"It's the best thing for my family."

Hogan blew smoke in my face and took a step closer to me. "The best thing for your family?" He repeated my words in his harsh, arctic tone. It wasn't sarcasm I heard in his voice, but something more sinister. *Contempt?*

"Mary Alice will be able to start over without a mountain of debt. The life insurance money will put Davis through college." I paused and felt my lip beginning to tremble. I bit down on it. "They'll both be better off without me."

"You're a fool," Hogan said, and disgust seemed to ooze from his whole being.

Again, I clenched my hands into fists. I didn't care if this man was a golfing legend anymore. *Where does he get off treating me—*

Hogan covered my fists with his hands and cut off my thoughts in an instant. I tried to wrangle away, but he was too strong. I remembered something I had heard Lee Trevino say about Hogan. That the man's wrists were so thick it was like his forearms went straight to his hands. Looking down at the man's huge paws now, I thought Trevino's words might be an understatement.

"Look at me," Hogan said.

The scent of disinfectant permeated my nostrils again. I didn't want to go back there. Anywhere but that hospital room. I felt like if I looked at Hogan's gray eyes, I was going to take another trip down memory lane, and I couldn't handle it.

"Do it," he instructed, squeezing my fists until I began to lose feeling in them.

"Please," I begged, but his voice became even harsher.

"*Do it.*"

Finally, as I felt the bones in both of my hands beginning to give way, I did as I was told. I peered into the eyes of Ben Hogan.

21

IT WAS AS IF MY BODY LEAPT RIGHT THROUGH HOGAN'S PU-
pils. I felt myself losing my balance, and I fell forward on my
knees. My hands, now free from the other man's grasp, lurched
forward and I caught myself on what felt like plywood floor-
ing. I took a deep breath and peered at my surroundings. I was
in the living room of a small house. I saw a man and a woman
arguing. The man looked a little like Ben Hogan, though he
was stockier, and his eyes were wide with anger. His demeanor
was a striking contrast to the icy cool of the man I had just been
talking to at Shady Oaks Country Club. What was this man
saying? Something about going back to work? Back to Dublin?
The words were coming to me as if they were being said under-
water, and I rubbed my ears. I rose to my feet and everything
came into better focus.

The room was tiny. There were a couple of chairs with a
coffee table in front of them. The man appeared to be gritting
his teeth, as the woman was saying that they needed to finish
out the school year. "For the kids' sake, Chester! Think of Royal
and Ben."

The man shook his head and gazed down at the floor. I followed his gaze and saw a newspaper lying on the table between the chairs. I leaned down to get a better look and read the words to myself: *Fort Worth Star-Telegram, Monday, February 13, 1922*.

I glanced back up at the couple. The woman was continuing to argue the virtues of staying in Fort Worth, but the man—Chester—didn't appear to be listening. He was holding a bag in his hand. Behind the couple, moving his eyes between them, was a young boy.

The man finally sighed and walked away from the woman. She called after him, but he ignored her. The boy followed, and I did as well. The man had entered a bedroom. He had set the bag on the bed and unzipped it. I peeked inside the bag, already knowing what would be there. Still, the sight of the black .38 caliber revolver made my breath catch in my throat.

Ben Hogan's father committed suicide . . .

It was part of the Hogan legend. No discussion of the quirky champion was complete without a mention of his father's suicide. Most biographers had included that Ben Hogan witnessed the act. I glanced from the gun back to the young boy, who had stopped in the opening of the doorway. He had a pensive look on his face, as if he wanted to tell his father something but didn't want to upset the man any further. *No*, I thought, examining the boy's T-shirt and tattered slacks. The tennis shoes he wore on his feet. *How old?* I wondered, trying to remember what I had read in the stories on Hogan. *Eight? Nine?*

I turned back to the man, and he was reaching for the gun. I watched as he gripped the weapon and gazed at himself across the room. There was a mirror, and I could see the reflection of Chester Hogan's gray eyes. They were the same color as his famous son's, but I didn't see the rigid firmness that I'd seen in the legendary golfer. This man looked lost. *Whipped*, as my father would say.

He brought the gun to his chest. "No!" I yelled, reaching my hand toward him. Then, not wanting to see, I turned to the boy. His own eyes had widened. His mouth hung open. The word *Dad* hung on his lips as he screamed, but I didn't hear the boy's voice.

It was drowned out by sound of the revolver firing behind me. I brought my hands to my ears, which were now ringing. The tone reminded me of the sound of the EKG machine when my son Graham had flatlined. I dropped to my knees, watching the terrified face of the boy. His mouth remained open, but his face had turned pale. Behind him, I saw the woman throw herself into the room and in front of the boy.

"Chester! Oh my God!" She turned around and looked at Ben, who continued to stand in the same spot. His expression had not changed.

Shock, I knew, feeling tears begin to stream down my face. *He's gone into shock.*

The woman screamed again and ran out of the room. "Ben, come out of here now. I'm going to call the police."

But the boy stayed put. He blinked a few times and gazed down at his unmoving father. Finally, the mother grabbed the boy around the arm and pulled him out of the room. I heard more screams and cries come from the living room, but the world was going dark. *What's happening?*

I couldn't see anything at all for a couple of seconds. "Mr. Hogan," I asked, but then I could see light again. I was in the same living room where Chester Hogan and his wife had been arguing before. I could see the woman standing at the front door. Through the window adjacent to the door, I saw several cars outside. The woman was wearing a long black dress.

"Ben, please come with us. We need to pay respects to your father."

The boy was sitting in one of the chairs. His arms were folded tight across his chest, and a scowl played over his face. He shook his head but didn't say anything.

The woman took a step closer. "Ben . . ." But then she sighed. "We'll be back in a few hours."

The boy said nothing as his mother opened the door and left the house. I went over to the other chair and sat down, watching the child. I saw his lip trembling and noticed that his hands were also shaking as he brought them to his face.

I reached my hand out and tried to place it on the boy's shoulder, but I felt nothing but air. *I'm a ghost.*

I leaned back in the chair and looked around the tiny house. *Nine years old*, I thought. *And he watched his father kill himself . . .*

Sighing, I rose from the chair and peered down at the boy. His hands still covered his face.

And now you're going to kill yourself, aren't you?

The older Ben Hogan's cold voice rang in my ear as I watched the nine-year-old version cry into his hands.

Finally, the boy's hands began to recede from his face. I gasped as I noticed that his features had changed. I was no longer looking at young Ben Hogan.

Instead, I was gazing down at the tear-streaked face of my daughter, Davis.

22

I WAS NO LONGER IN BEN HOGAN'S CHILDHOOD HOME. IN-
stead, I was sitting in a white wrought-iron chair at a small
circular table. My daughter was wearing a long, black dress.
Her eyes were red-rimmed, and her nose was running. She was
twelve years old.

I knew this setting well. The table was smack in the middle
of a small kitchen. I had spent many a morning drinking coffee
with my mother here in the two years since my father had
passed. And now I saw her. She was standing by the stove, using
a knife to cut a piece of pie. Her hair was colored a dark red,
which had been her preference once her natural brown locks
had turned gray. She put the sliver of pie on a plate and placed it
in front of Davis. "Egg custard pie makes everything better,"
she said, and I heard her voice crack ever so slightly. She snatched
a Kleenex from a box on the counter and handed it to Davis.
"Wipe your nose, honey." She forced a smile, but Davis's face
didn't change. She dabbed her nose and crinkled up the tissue.
Then she gazed at the wall, ignoring the dessert in front of her.

Mom, who was sitting in the chair next to Davis, reached forward and grabbed my daughter's hand. "You need to eat something, honey."

"Not hungry," she said.

"Your momma says you've barely eaten a thing since your brother . . ." Again, Mom's voice cracked, and I looked away, not wanting to see her or Davis in pain. *Where was I while this was going on?* I wondered. I didn't remember going over to Mom's house on the day of the funeral, which, based on Davis's attire, this had to be.

Why am I being shown this?

"I wish it was me," Davis said, and the bitterness in her voice drew my eyes back to her.

"Don't *ever* say that, honey," Mom said, and her tone was firm, the crack long gone.

"I do," Davis said. "Graham was a lot better person than me. He was smarter. He was a better athlete." She paused, and her voice shook with emotion. "Everyone loved him. Even me." Davis wiped her eyes and looked at Mom. "I loved him a lot."

"I know, honey." She scooted her chair around to Davis and wrapped an arm around her. "I know."

"I never told him," Davis said. "I never told my brother that I loved him until he got sick. Can you believe that? I was too cool to say it."

"He knew you loved him."

"I should have told him. I should have told him every day."

I heard the sound of a voice clearing behind me, and I wheeled out of my chair toward it. My father, Robert Clark, was standing in the doorway between the kitchen and the den. He wore a black suit, white shirt, and maroon tie. His face was pale, and his shoulders were stooped. He looked smaller than I remembered him. *How long has he been standing there?*

"People never say everything they should to the people they love," Dad said, and the sound of his gravelly voice seemed to startle Mom and Davis. They both turned to look up at him. "None of us do," Dad continued, approaching the table and taking the seat I had just vacated. When he sighed, I could feel the pain in the room. This was my family, and I remembered now.

Mary Alice and I had stayed behind at the cemetery. We had asked Mom and Dad to take Davis to their house. We had both wanted some time with Graham's casket. Mary Alice had alternated between fits of anger and stoic silence as we had mourned our son. Finally, we both had put our hands on his grave and she had prayed to God that our son was with Jesus and that his suffering was over. I had taken her home, then gone over to Mom and Dad's to pick up Davis. While we were gone, this scene must have been playing out.

"I miss him, Pawpaw," Davis said, bringing me back to the moment.

"Me too, sweetheart." He ran a hand through Davis's hair.

"And I'm worried about Mom and Dad. They're both trying to be strong and all, but I know they are dying inside."

I felt my eyes begin to water, and then I let the tears fall. "They'll be okay, Davis. Your momma's a tough woman, and she puts her faith in God. She'll get through this."

"What about Dad?"

My father stood from the table and walked back to the door leading out to the den. "Davis, I want you to remember something about your daddy," he said, as he placed his hand on the door.

I felt my heartbeat flutter as I turned to my daughter. "What's that?" Davis asked.

I moved my eyes to Dad, who was now looking over his shoulder at Davis. "Your daddy is stronger than all of us."

I took a step backward so that I could now see them both. I was in utter shock at what my father had said. "Even you?" Davis asked, and a tiny smile came to her face.

"Especially me," Dad said, and then he walked out of the kitchen.

23

I GAZED DUMBFOUNDED AT THE CLOSED DOOR. THEN I glanced down at the table, where Davis was eating her first bite of pie.

"That's my grandgirl," Mom said, kissing her on the cheek. My heart swelled as I watched my mother, Elizabeth Lowe Clark, dote on my grieving daughter. The one person who had always made me feel better about any situation was Mom. Whether it was a skinned knee, a bad golf round, or a poor grade, Mom never made me feel anything but loved. It was her gift.

I wiped the tears from my face and walked unsteadily toward the door that led out of the kitchen. I was hoping to see where my father had gone. But when I opened the door, I was no longer in my parents' house.

I was standing beneath a tree and looking into the tense eyes of Ben Hogan. He released his grip on my hands, and I stumbled backward a few steps. For a long moment, I stared at him, unsure of what to say or where to even begin. Mercifully, Ben broke the silence.

"I'm sorry about your son."

"Thank you," I said, holding his gaze. "I'm sorry about your dad." I paused. "You saw it happen. I can't imagine . . ." I trailed off, because I was telling the truth. I couldn't imagine what it would have been like for him to watch his father kill himself. *But yet he had survived. And thrived. Ben Hogan became one of the greatest golfers in the history of the sport.* I looked at the ghost standing beside the tree. "Do you think watching your dad kill himself made you who you became?"

"And who was that?"

I smiled. "Ben Hogan. One of the greatest players to ever live. Winner of nine major championships."

He squinted at me. "I don't know. Some folks think it made me reclusive and antisocial. Others said it made me mean."

"Did it?"

He continued to squint at me. "Life has many mysteries."

"What kind of answer is that?"

"A truthful one."

I started to respond but stopped myself. I was curious about something else. "Why did you show me the interaction with Mom, Dad, and Davis after Graham's funeral?"

Hogan turned away from me and grabbed the seven iron he'd leaned against the tree. He rolled another ball into the long divot. Before taking his stance, he peered at me. "What did you see?"

I took a tentative step toward him and rubbed my hand over my face. "They were upset. Mom had made Davis a pie, and she was crying. And Dad . . ." I stopped and glared at him. "What do you mean, what did I see? You know what I saw. What would you call it?"

"Pain," Ben said, taking his stance and, after waiting a few seconds to eye the target, making another swing. This shot landed a couple of feet left of the chair. "A lot of pain," he added. Then he gazed at me. "You weren't the only one who was affected by your son's death. Your daughter. Your wife. Your mom." He paused. "And your father."

"I know that," I said, hearing the exasperation in my voice.

"Do you? Could've fooled me. Do you suspect that any of them are about to take their own life?"

"Dad's life has already been taken," I snapped.

"I know and I'm sorry. But what about your wife and daughter. And your mom? They are all still dealing with the pain, aren't they?"

"I know," I said, turning away from him and looking out at the green, flat fairways of Shady Oaks.

"So?"

I sighed. "It's different for me. I owe a ton of money. Hundreds of thousands of dollars. My marriage has been suffocated by Graham's death and all the hospital debt. And Davis isn't going to have much of a future if I can't send her to college. And Mom . . ." I felt a lump in my chest, remembering the scene I had just witnessed at my mother's house after Graham's funeral and how tender Mom had been with Davis. I was all she had left. How would she react to my suicide? "Mom will understand that I did what I had to do," I managed, hoping my words were true.

Ben scoffed. "And so jumping off the Tennessee River Bridge is going to solve all those problems for you?"

I nodded. "With the life insurance money, Mary Alice can pay off all of the hospital debt and put Davis through college. The sooner I'm gone, the quicker and easier it will be for both of them to move on with their lives. And they'll be able to do it free and clear of any debt . . . and free and clear of me."

"Do you really believe there's no future for you?" Ben asked. He had lit another cigarette and, after retrieving a bucket from under the tree, had walked about ten yards down the fairway toward the chair that he'd been using as a target. "You truly believe that you are out of options?" he asked, more loudly than he had before.

"I've got nothing left to give." I paused. "Except my life."

Ben continued to walk down the fairway, and I followed him. I was beginning to wonder what the deal was here. Unlike the dream with Bobby Jones and Johnnie, my clubs hadn't mysteriously appeared. Hogan, for his part, only seemed to have one club with him and was on a random hole in the middle of the golf course. I trotted to catch up and cleared my throat. "Mr. Hogan, are we going to play any holes? I was under the impression that we'd be playing."

"No," he said without elaboration. His gait had slowed, and I noticed that he was limping.

"Are you okay?" I asked.

When we reached the chair, Hogan plopped down in the seat. He sighed and took a long drag off his cigarette. "I'm tired, boy." Then he pulled up his pant legs to his knees and I saw the tape that covered each leg.

I peered at him. "Why do you still need tape on your legs? You're . . . a ghost now."

"Do you know why my legs are covered"—he pointed down at his ankles—"with this mess?"

I nodded. Though I wasn't as familiar with the part of the Hogan legend involving his father's suicide, every serious golf fan knew why Ben Hogan had difficulty walking in the latter part of his career. "You were in a car crash. A Greyhound bus heading in the opposite direction as your vehicle was making a pass on a two-lane road on a foggy night. The driver must not have seen you, and the bus hit your car head-on. At the last possible moment, you covered your wife's body with your own. You saved her life."

"And my own," Hogan said, wincing and rubbing his hands up and down his taped legs.

"You broke every bone in your body, didn't you?"

"Not quite," he said. "But almost."

"I watched the movie. I can't remember the name of it, but Glenn Ford played you."

Hogan winced again. Then he peered up at me with a gaze that could have pierced glass. "Randy, do you think you're the only one who's ever been dealt a bad hand in life?"

"No," I said, looking away from him. "No, I'm not saying that at all."

"Then why are you quitting?"

My arms tensed with anger, but I still could not meet his stare. "Because it's the best option for my family. It solves our financial problems, and Davis and Mary Alice will have a chance at a future."

"Even if you are right and your wife and daughter do carve out a future"—he paused and puffed on his cigarette—"they'd give anything in the world to have you back." Ben's voice had grown quieter and more reflective. I finally peered down at him, but now he was looking up at the sky.

"How do you know that?"

"Because I would have given anything to have another hour with my father."

I swallowed hard and again looked away from him. I gave my head a jerk and let out a deep breath. "I've been over it all a million times, Mr. Hogan. The only choice I have that will solve my family's problems is to jump off that bridge."

"No," he snapped.

I glared down at him, and his steel-gray eyes were locked onto mine. "What do you mean, *no*? How in the world do you know anything about me?"

"Not the only choice," he said, his voice as cold as the inside of a freezer. "The *easiest*."

"Go to hell," I said, and my voice had begun to shake with anger.

He smiled, but his eyes remained humorless. After another drag on the cigarette, he extended his hand. "Here, help me up."

I reached down and grasped Hogan's right hand. When I felt the rough, hard hand envelop my own, I wondered if he'd tricked me into taking another trip down memory lane. I closed my eyes and waited for the ground to open beneath me. What was I going to see? The bus crash itself? The aftermath in the hospital? Another scene from my own life? *Please no . . .*

"No," Hogan said, and my eyes flew open. I had gone nowhere. Hogan stood before me and pushed his cap up a centimeter. "No more trips with me. I'm done. You need to toughen up, Clark. Life isn't easy on any of us. Whether it's a bus crash or watching your own father kill himself, all people experience pain in this cruel world, and some have to endure more of it than others." He paused and leaned closer to me. Though the man was smaller than me in height and weight, I felt myself cowering.

"How?" I asked. The word just kind of popped out of my mouth. "What can I do?"

His gaze narrowed. "You keep going," he said. "To conquer pain, you have to be resilient and keep pushing forward."

"I've tried," I said. "For three years, I've tried to get past it, but the debt keeps mounting and I just . . . hate myself."

"You have gifts, Randy. Things that you can do."

"I can't hit a golf ball like you."

He finally smiled. "No, you can't. But you have other talents."

I shook my head. "None that are going to dig me out of this hole."

He let go of my hand. The smile was gone. "Yes, you do. You just don't have the guts to use them."

My eyes widened.

"You aren't hearing anything that I or Mr. Jones have told you."

"Yes, I have. Self-control and resilience. In order to survive what I'm going through, I need both qualities. Jones learned to control his temper and became a great champion. You were resilient enough to recover from your father's suicide and getting run over by a bus." I sighed. "I get it. I really do. My situation is different."

"No," he snapped. "It's not."

Before I could respond, he grabbed me up under the armpits and shook me. His hands were unbelievably strong . . . I tried to move, but I couldn't budge. I was powerless to do anything but stare into his gray eyes.

"How did the son of Robert Clark become such a whiner?"

I glared at him. "Did you know my father?"

"I know everything about you." He shook me hard and my head jostled. I was beginning to get dizzy.

"Then you know the deal. My father never believed in me. Never said one word of encouragement my whole life."

"Mine shot himself in the chest." Hogan's voice was just above a whisper. "Every person has to deal with stuff, Randy. You aren't going to hurt your father by jumping off that bridge.

He's dead. The only folks that get hurt are your wife and daughter, and anyone else you might have helped with your God-given talents. Is that what you want?"

I blinked, but no words would come.

"Is that what you want?" he repeated, his words now louder. So loud that my eardrums hurt. He shook me again, and I felt my feet lifting off the ground. I looked down at him, and he had a scowl of fury on his face.

"Get out of my sight," he said, and let go of my arms. I braced for impact with the ground, hoping I didn't separate a shoulder, but I landed on my back. I felt the wind go out of me, and I struggled for breath. When I was able to let out a few ragged breaths, I rolled over to a sitting position and looked up at the figure who had just thrown me down like a rag doll.

But the ghost of Ben Hogan was gone. I climbed to my feet, wiping the grass and dirt off my backside. Through the dim rays of the setting sun, I saw that I was back on the driving range at Shoal Creek. Shady Oaks was gone. Hogan was gone.

I took in a deep breath and slowly exhaled. My chest ached from the fall I had taken, and I could still hear Hogan's voice chiming in my ears. *Is that what you want?*

"You okay, Mr. Clark?"

I pivoted at the sound of the voice and saw the kid who had guided me to the locker room a few hours earlier, who had told me a man named Ben was waiting for me out by the range.

"Is your friend gone?" he asked.

I nodded.

He scratched his head. "We're about to shut things down. Want me to have your car brought around?"

I peered behind me at the expanse of the driving range and then the undulating terrain of Shoal Creek, which was such a contrast to the flat fairways of Shady Oaks. "Yeah," I managed. "That would be good."

"You sure you're okay, Mr. Clark? Your face is white as a sheet."

Wincing as I took in another breath, I smiled at him. "I'm fine, kid. Just bring the car. Thanks."

He gave me a salute and ran off down the cart path that led to the clubhouse. I followed after him, my legs rubbery. I was exhausted. I glanced at my watch. It was almost seven o'clock, and I had a two-hour drive in front of me.

When I reached the clubhouse, I looked over my shoulder at the driving range. Darkness had now made its final descent, and I could barely see anything other than the shadows of the tree limbs. Then my heart caught in my throat as the silhouette of a person slowly came into view. He had to be leaning against a tree, though all I could make out was the shadow of the man and his Ben Hogan cap.

I saw a spark of light and knew that he had lit another cigarette.

Is that what you want? Despite the almost three hundred yards between us, it was as if he were whispering from a foot away. Then, just like that, the light from his match flickered out and there was only darkness.

THIRD ROUND

24

I WOKE UP THE NEXT MORNING SLUGGISH AND THIRSTY. I HAD arrived home the previous night at nine thirty and slept on the couch in the den, since Mary Alice was still under the weather. Before attempting to sleep, I had watched the Masters highlights on CBS. Seve Ballesteros from Spain, a two-time Masters champion and probably the best player in the world, had vaulted to the lead with a second-round sixty-eight. That didn't bother me, because I liked Ballesteros and his bold brand of play. Jack had played better, firing a seventy-one, and was now one over for the tourney. He had made the cut, so he'd be around for the weekend. But he was still six shots behind Ballesteros, and based on the highlights, it was hard to imagine Seve faltering.

I barely slept a wink all night, haunted by the silhouetted image of Ben Hogan leaning against the tree and lighting his cigarette, whispering over and over again, *Is that what you want? Is that what you want?*

I poured myself a tall glass of ice water and drained it in one gulp. I had driven home from Shoal Creek in a daze and had forgotten to eat or drink anything.

After downing a second glass of water, I noticed an open box of Cap'n Crunch that Davis must have left on the counter after coming home late. I normally ate Raisin Bran, but what the heck? I fixed myself a bowl of the sweetened corn concoction and splashed a little milk on top.

"Breakfast of champions, I see?"

I looked up to see my wife dressed in her white bathrobe with the initials *MADC* embroidered in red across the front.

"Mary Alice Davis Clark," I said, winking at her. "Aren't you a sight?"

Her hair was a tousled mess and her skin was pale, but her tired smile and soft touch on my shoulder sent a tingle of warmth through my body. "How was Charlotte?" she asked, sitting down next to me.

After another spoonful of cereal, I said, "She's holding up okay. I think she's more angry than sad."

"The stages of grief," Mary Alice said, shaking her head. "Want me to make you some coffee? My stomach is too weak, but—"

"No, I'm good. I'll make some in a minute. Here, sit down. Why don't you let me fix you something?"

She sat heavily in the seat next to mine and began to rub her knuckles over her temples.

"You might be dehydrated," I said. "Do we have any Gatorade?"

She shook her head and winced. "No, but I think there's a Sprite in the fridge."

I grabbed the last remaining Sprite from a six-pack in the refrigerator and poured it over ice in a glass. Then I took the box of Cap'n Crunch and emptied out a few pieces of the cereal into a bowl, forgoing any milk. "Here, why don't you try to eat a little of this? Should be pretty bland without the milk."

She smiled up at me and picked up one of the small, square morsels between her fingers, hesitated for a moment, and then stuck it into her mouth. She chewed slowly and took a tiny sip of her drink. "Well, it's official. I'm never eating my mother's cooking again."

I laughed, and it felt good to laugh. Here we were, a woman whose mother had almost killed her with meat loaf and a man contemplating suicide who'd just buried his best friend, sharing a breakfast of Cap'n Crunch. It wasn't necessarily a Hallmark card, but it felt good. The best I'd felt in a long time.

"I think I'd like to go see Graham today," she said. Her voice was hoarse from all the vomiting, but there was also the ever-present despair that I heard every time she mentioned our son's name.

The stages of grief, I thought, echoing my wife's words from a moment ago. Denial, anger, bargaining, depression and, finally, acceptance. The last one, at least for my wife and me, seemed beyond all reach.

Any good vibes that had begun to sprout died. "Okay," I whispered. "When?"

"After I take a shower," she said.

"Do you want me to go with you?" I felt obligated to ask. In the first few months after Graham's death, we had always visited his grave site together. We both would cry and hold each other. Mary Alice was inconsolable in those days, and it was all I could do to get her to leave. She would plant kisses on the marker and get down on her knees and give it a hug. Over time, I couldn't bear to watch anymore. Eventually, Mary Alice started visiting the cemetery alone.

"No," she said. "Unless you want to."

The words hung in the air for several seconds. Finally, I rose from the table and stuck my empty cereal bowl in the sink. "I should probably swing by the office. No telling what was dumped on my desk yesterday while I was gone."

She nodded and lifted another piece of Cap'n Crunch to her mouth. I saw a lone teardrop slide down her cheek, which she made no move to wipe away.

I washed out the bowl with soap and water and turned to leave. I kissed her cheek where the tear had now dried. "I hope you feel better."

As I walked away, her hoarse voice called from behind me. "Randy."

She was looking up at me with a question in her brown eyes. She was beautiful in the morning light that was now cascading in from the window above the kitchen sink.

"What?" I asked.

After a second's hesitation, the question in her gaze dissipated. "Nothing."

25

I HAVEN'T BEEN TO MY SON'S GRAVE IN OVER A YEAR. Even as I have contemplated ending my own life, I have not been able to bring myself to go back there. Does this make me feel guilty? Yes. Do I feel like I'm less of a man? Less of a human being because I can't endure the despair that his place in the cemetery brings? Yes, across the board.

But yet I don't go and won't go. I prefer to watch the old videos I have of us as a family, though I rarely even do that anymore. All these glimpses of my boy onscreen do is bring more pain. His smiling face, in mid-laugh at something his sister has said and done, is like sharp nails raking down the chalkboard of my heart.

I can't take it anymore. I can't take the anguish in my wife's voice and face. I can't take the fact that there is nothing I can do to ease her pain and despair. I can't take the sense that I have no control over what has happened to me.

I can't bring Graham back. I can't pay his hospital bills. I can't provide a future for Mary Alice or Davis.

All I can do is jump . . .

AFTER SLIPPING ON A PAIR OF KHAKI PANTS, GOLF SHIRT, AND sweater, I headed out the door with my briefcase in hand. I paused in the doorway and said good-bye to my wife, and she yelled a "be careful" as the door closed behind me. For as long as I've known her, Mary Alice has told me to "be careful" every time I go anywhere. It's one of those endearing motherly things that Davis rolls her eyes at, but that I know also brings her comfort. If Mary Alice Clark didn't tell me to "be careful" before I walked out the door, I would think I was in some alternate universe.

As I walked to my car, I saw no sign of Davis's Jeep. "Goose Pond," I said out loud, feeling a flutter in my stomach. Davis and the Huntsville High women's golf team were in Scottsboro playing in a regional invitational. It was the biggest event of the season so far.

And I forgot our ritual . . .

Before every tournament, Davis and I always went over her plan for the round. Each tee shot. The side of the fairway she wanted to be on. The type of greens and how they would putt. I had played Goose Pond numerous times and could have helped her. Usually, we had this discussion over dinner the night before the tourney. When she was younger, I would drive her to tournaments and caddy for her. In those days, our planning sessions were fun and exciting and would sometimes carry over to the course. But since her brother's death, Davis and I both seemed to merely be going through the motions for the sake of tradition.

Sometimes if I had to work late the evening before an event, she would wake me up the next morning to review her plan.

But not today . . .

This was the first time we failed to even attempt the ritual. She left without a peep, and I wasn't even able to wish her luck.

As I climbed into my car, a dagger of remorse cut through me. *I'm failing her,* I thought. *Just like I'm failing her mother.*

"Please God, let her play well," I whispered, as I turned the key. I almost laughed at the absurdity of me praying for my daughter to shoot a good score on the golf course while I was still seriously considering ending my own life. For that matter, praying at all seemed a bit hypocritical given my lack of faith in the Almighty these days.

I sighed as I backed out of the driveway. I glanced at the briefcase that I had flung onto the floorboard, wondering if there was any point in going into the office. *What the heck?* I thought. *Where else am I gonna go?* I didn't want to go to the club. The last two times I had been to a golf course, I'd suffered through hallucinations that had taken me to East Lake Golf Club in Atlanta, Georgia, in the 1920s and Shady Oaks Country Club in Fort Worth, Texas, circa 1960. For a second, I pondered whether to again try to drive to Decatur and finish things once and for all with a plunge off the Tennessee River Bridge. But after tossing and turning all night with the ghost of Ben Hogan in my ear, jumping to my doom didn't sound right.

Was I having doubts? I guess I was.

"The office it is," I said out loud.

26

THE FIRM WAS A DARK AND LONELY PLACE ON SATURDAY
morning. As I trudged down the empty hallway to my office,
I was struck by the stark quiet that surrounded me. It was like
visiting the fairgrounds the day after the carnival had left town.
The constant ringing of telephones and rapid clicking of keys
was gone. As was the chatter by the coffeepot and the muf-
fled sounds of talking behind closed conference room doors. I
avoided working at the office on the weekends, preferring to
bring a few files home if I absolutely had to work. But sometimes, especially if I was getting ready for a trial, it was neces-
sary to come in. Normally, I would turn on a few lights, but I
didn't feel like it today. I stepped into my office and sat down in
the high-backed burgundy chair that the firm had given me as a
gift when I'd started thirteen years earlier. At the time, I'd been
proud of the large power chair where I would take phone calls
and prepare for trials. Now, as I sat down, I only felt silly. This
squeaky artifact of the golden age of law was uncomfortable and
ridiculous. I sank down in it and gazed around the dark room.

The only light came from my window that looked out over Spragins Street below. It cast a glow over the portrait of the thirteenth green at Augusta National that hung on the far wall.

I stared at the painting, thinking back to a couple nights earlier, when the ghost of Darby Hays and I had both hit shots into that green.

What is happening to me? I wondered, thinking through everything that had transpired since I turned forty on Wednesday. Ben Hogan's words rang in my ears.

You aren't going to hurt your father by jumping off that bridge. He's dead. The only folks that get hurt are your wife and daughter, and anyone else you might have helped with your God-given talents. Is that what you want?

"I don't know," I said out loud. I felt my heartbeat beginning to race and I stood up from the chair, bracing my hands on my desk. "I don't know!" I screamed the words and had a vision of my wife kneeling by my son's grave, caressing the concrete and kissing the words written on it. *Robert Graham Clark II.*

We had named him after my father. It had been Mary Alice's idea, since we had used her maiden name for Davis.

The two people who had hurt me the most in life shared the same name. Dad had a million chances to change things but hadn't.

And Graham had been given no chance at all. There was no explanation from some higher power as to why my son was taken. He just was.

I felt hot tears streaking down my cheek. I glanced up at the portrait of Augusta and wanted to throw something at it. I wanted to break everything in the office. I wanted to pull all of my hair out and beat my face with my fists until I couldn't feel anything anymore.

I want to jump.

"I want to jump." I repeated the words out loud, but they didn't sound strong. *How did the son of Robert Clark become such a whiner?*

Hogan again. I pressed my hands against the sides of my head and pushed, trying to rid my brain of that arctic, unsympathetic voice. As I focused my eyes in the dark, I now heard more voices.

You're fighting awful hard to stay on this bridge for someone planning to jump.

You need to toughen up, Clark . . . all people experience pain in this cruel world . . .

Your daddy is stronger than all of us . . .

I groaned and shook my head against the sounds. *I'm losing my mind.*

I staggered away from the desk and saw a Post-it note lying on the floor. I snatched it up and read the words out loud, trying to force out the other voices. *Ellie Timberlake called. Wants to have lunch next week to discuss something. Wouldn't say what it was about.*

I blinked at the words scribbled on the note. Eleanor Timberlake was a sixty-two-year-old solo practitioner. She specialized in personal-injury plaintiff's cases and had obtained the largest verdict in Madison County history by a female attorney a decade earlier. I had tangled with Ellie, as she liked to be called, or "Ms. Ellie," as everyone in the bar referred to her, in at least ten depositions and they had all been knock-down, drag-out affairs. Ellie Timberlake was ruthless and as warm and fuzzy as a box of nails. The only somewhat nice moment I'd ever had with her was when she agreed to a continuance of a trial because of Graham's death.

Ellie was the sole female plaintiff's lawyer in Huntsville. I had been both flattered and afraid when she'd asked me four years ago to become her law partner. I had taken only one plaintiff's case in my ten-year career up to that point, and I'd worried about it nonstop. Whether I had pleaded the proper claims, whether I had the correct names of the defendants listed, whether the type of service of process was sufficient, and so on. Even when I finally settled the case for a nice payday for my client and the firm, I was stricken by whether the confidentiality agreement I'd advised my client to sign was sound and whether the release was too broad. In summary, I didn't think plaintiff's work was for me.

I mentioned all these things during my meeting with Ellie, and she brushed them off as "defense lawyer fears." "My line of work is a volume business, Randy. You can't just have one case. You'll worry it to death, and let's face it, we plaintiff's lawyers are like batters in baseball. Even the good ones"—she had smiled—"like me are lucky to hit over three hundred in front of a jury. We're gonna lose some cases, but you have to be willing to go the distance and lose in order to have any chance at a big settlement. That takes time, and I've paid my dues. What I need now is a partner. How does Timberlake and Clark sound?"

I must have appeared shocked by her request, because she had laughed out loud. "Think about it, Randy. If you don't jump off the insurance-defense treadmill at some point, you're gonna wake up and be my age and never realize your full potential as a lawyer."

"Do you have to be a plaintiff's lawyer to fulfill your potential?" I had asked, my voice incredulous.

"Not at all. But you're trapped in your current gig. Every defense lawyer I know is fussing about how the insurance companies are cutting their time and hampering their trial strategies."

I had bitten my lip and not responded, but I knew she was right. Still, the insurers I worked for were reliable clients who paid their bills. I wasn't going to get rich working for them, but I would be able to eat.

Ellie had closed the meeting by saying something that I'd never forgotten, and that occasionally kept me up at night in the weeks after making my decision. "I've taken a lot of cases to a jury verdict, Randy, and you're one of a handful of defense lawyers who bring out the best in me. I know that if I don't bring my A game, you're going to whip my butt." She had smiled as she rose from her seat. "It's time for me to take on a partner, and my first choice is you."

I had told Ellie that I would think about her offer, and I did think. I thought hard, and a couple of times I had almost been about to pick up the phone and say yes. I had spoken with Dad about Ellie's proposal, and he wasn't keen on it. *You've got a steady job with a good firm working for solid clients. What more do you want? Do you really want to be an ambulance chaser?*

I had protested, as I always did when Dad provided the voice of logic and reason, but his words had sunk in. I'd talked with Mary Alice, who also didn't like the idea of me leaving a stable job for something completely unknown. *How much do you know about Ellie Timberlake? What if she treats you like a hired hand? What if she stiffs you on your share of the pie?*

I had heard plenty of war stories about plaintiff's firms breaking up over the division of fees on settlements and verdicts, and Mary Alice's fears struck a chord. She had tried to let me down easy, but in the end, she was scared of losing what we had. *Why don't you wait until things are a little calmer? We can't afford any loss of income, can we? Why don't you wait a few years and then think about making a move? Maybe when the kids are finished with high school?*

There was one other concern, and it dwarfed anything that Mary Alice or Dad had said.

What if I wasn't good enough?

Deep down, I wasn't sure I had the stuff to tee it up as a plaintiff's lawyer week in and week out. I knew that the court-houses were littered with personal injury plaintiff's lawyers who didn't have a pot to pee in. I wouldn't simply be earning a modest paycheck anymore, nor would I be working for an in-surance company that paid my hourly rate. In the plaintiff's world, you ate what you killed. If you didn't win or settle the case, you didn't bring home anything.

Despite what Ellie had told me, I wasn't sure I could handle the pressure of a full-time career of suing other people and companies for money. If I failed, it wasn't just my career on the line. It was my children's futures. It was the life that Mary Alice and I had built together. Was I willing to risk what I had for the prospect of something better? What if I failed? Could I deal with that?

Was I good enough?

I had finally told Ellie Timberlake that I couldn't do it. She had not protested. Instead, she had simply grunted and said, "Okay." Then she had hung up the phone before I could say anything further. A short while later, she had taken on a young female partner named Glenda Yates. I hadn't exactly followed whether the new partnership had been successful. I still had a number of cases with Ellie, but she never mentioned how she and Yates were doing or anything about the offer that I had refused. I figured she had written me off.

What does she want now? I wondered, gazing at the handwritten note my secretary had taken. We had several cases going right now, including one set for trial in ninety days. There was also the opening on the bench. Judge Douglas Brinkley was stepping down at the end of the year, and folks were beginning to announce their intention to run for his spot. She might be rounding up support for her candidacy, though that didn't seem right. Ellie was too adversarial to be a judge, but who knew? Maybe she'd finally gotten tired of trying cases.

I crumpled up the note and tossed it into the center of my desk.

I guess it doesn't matter, I thought, gazing back at the portrait of the thirteenth hole of Augusta on the wall. *If I jump, nothing is going to matter.*

I sighed and closed my eyes. I was so tired. For a moment, I thought again of Mary Alice, sitting on the ground in front of Graham's grave. Then, ever so faintly, I heard the far-off patter of what sounded like . . .

. . . *clapping?*

I opened my eyes and started to walk across the office to the window overlooking Spragins Street. There were probably some kids playing down below.

But I stopped dead still when I glanced at the painting of the thirteenth hole at Augusta.

The green didn't have four bunkers surrounding it anymore, nor did I see the clusters of red azaleas. Instead, there was a bunker in front of the green and I was gazing backward up a fairway. And there were people in the picture now. A gallery?

Yes, there was a gallery of folks that lined both sides of the fairway. I walked closer to the painting, and the clapping sound grew louder. I took another step, and the sound grew almost deafening.

"Randy," I heard someone say, and took yet another step. I was a foot away from the picture. I reached toward the people I saw and could now make out their clothing. The men wore slacks and golf shirts, and the women had on sundresses. As I touched the painting, I felt fingers grasp my own and pull me forward.

27

I WAS NOW STANDING IN THE PAINTING. I WAS ON A GOLF course. My eyes widened, and my pulse quickened. Several people were now looking at me and shooting me ugly looks.

"I'm sorry," I whispered. I started to look around, and then I felt my hand being squeezed. "Johnnie?" It was the Scotsman who had caddied for me and Bobby Jones in my round at East Lake.

"Aye," he said. Then, smiling, he pointed at the swell of people. "Look."

I followed his index finger and my breath caught in my throat as I took in the scene. From our perch on a hill above the green, I saw an incredible mass of people that must have been six rows deep on each side of the fairway. The mob had swelled to ten deep around the green. I glanced to my right and saw a scoreboard. The top of it read *1960 United States Open*.

Sweet mother of G . . .

I didn't complete the thought as my eardrums began to throb with more clapping, followed by whistles and a few screams of "There he is! Yeah!"

I blinked and subconsciously a grin came to my face as I recognized the figure stalking down the fairway toward the green. He wore a short-sleeve collared shirt and tailored pants and walked with a forward lean. I could see the tight sinewy muscles in the man's arms and noticed a cigarette dangling from the corner of his mouth. A few steps before he reached the green, the man reached behind him and hitched up the back of his pants.

"By God," I said, hearing the awe in my own voice. "It's Arnold Palmer."

"Aye," Johnnie said.

It was a breathtaking scene to be in the midst of "Arnie's Army," the nickname bestowed upon the fans who followed Arnold's every move on the golf course. "What round is this?" I asked, gazing down at Johnnie.

"The finish of the third."

I rubbed my chin and thought it through. If this was the 1960 U.S. Open, then I was at Cherry Hills Country Club on the outskirts of Denver.

"Arnold wins this tournament," I whispered.

But Johnnie said nothing. We watched Arnold and his playing partner putt out on the green, and then they pushed through the crowd toward what must have been a scorer's tent. Now that his round had concluded, the people around us had begun to mingle and I caught snippets of the conversations.

"He's seven shots back."

"Not even Arnold can come back from that."

"My money's on Hogan. He hasn't been close in years, and he wants this one bad."

"What about the fat kid from Ohio who hits the ball a mile?"

I nudged Johnnie with my elbow and winked at him. "The fat kid they're talking about is Jack Nicklaus."

Johnnie peered up at me as if I had expelled gas and he was trying hard not to smell it. "Aye. I know that, Randy."

"Right," I said, rubbing my hands together. "So . . . what now? What am I supposed to see here?"

Johnnie smiled and showed off a row of crooked teeth. "How about a bevvie?" he asked.

"A what?"

"A drink. A shot of Scotch whiskey or some such. Whatever your pleasure."

I gazed around the tournament grounds, looking for a tent that served alcohol. "Sounds good, but I don't see . . ."

"Not out here, silly man. In there." He pointed at the Tudor-style clubhouse, which had a slight resemblance to East Lake.

I smiled down at him. "Really?"

"Aye. Don't you want to see the makings of a legend?"

THE NINETEENTH-HOLE LOUNGE AT CHERRY HILLS WAS A hodgepodge of smells. Hamburger and hot dog meat, grease and beer, all laced with cigarette and cigar smoke that hung in the air. Johnnie and I walked past a few tables to the bar, where he ordered a Dewar's and water and I said I'd have the same. "Can he see us?" I asked Johnnie while peering at the bartender.

"Aye," Johnnie said, taking the drinks. "But only long enough to pour us our whiskey. Now we've disappeared."

"How's that?" I asked, waving my hands at the bartender, who, sure enough, acted as if I weren't there anymore.

"Got me, Randy. I don't make the rules here. I just play by them."

That didn't make much sense, but I was too intrigued by the

surroundings to care. There, in the corner of the lounge, Arnold Palmer was sitting alone. "Can we . . . ?"

"Come on," Johnnie said, gesturing for me to follow him. "You're going to want to see this."

We approached Arnold and took seats at the table next to him. Arnold appeared to be lost in his own thoughts, probably going over the previous round in his mind. It was odd to see the King like this. The only times I'd ever seen Arnold Palmer in person were when he was signing autographs at Augusta, and he was always so talkative and friendly. Here, he looked withdrawn and intense. A young waitress brought over a plate of food and held a drink in her hand. "Cheeseburger, fries, and a half lemonade . . . half sweet tea, Mr. Palmer."

"Yes, ma'am," Arnold said, winking at her as she placed his food on the table. As she turned away, the waitress's face had turned pink and a tiny grin played on her face.

"Awesome," I whispered, not sure if it was cooler to see the man take a sip of the drink that would one day bear his name or how he had made a total stranger blush with a simple wink.

"Aye," Johnnie whispered back. "Awesome."

Arnold ate a few bites from his cheeseburger and then called out to one of the men at the next table. "Hey, Bob. How far do you think a sixty-five will take me this afternoon?"

Bob smiled and blew a cloud of cigar smoke in the air. "Nowhere," he said.

I turned back to Arnold and saw his face darken. "What do you say, Dan?" Arnold asked, shifting his gaze to the other man at the table, who looked familiar. *Dan Jenkins*, I thought, snapping my fingers and glancing at Johnnie, who nodded. Dan had a thatch of brown hair on top of his head and a gleam in his eyes. The best part of my *Sports Illustrated* subscription was reading Dan's articles. "You're seven shots back, Arnie . . ." He trailed off and took a bite from a French fry.

"You guys are crazy," Arnold said, forcing a laugh, but his voice was defiant. "Two eighty always wins the Open, and that's what sixty-five would give me for the tourney. Isn't that right, Bob?"

Bob slid his plate out of the way and leaned forward on his elbows. "Shoot sixty-five. Don't shoot it. Won't make any difference. You don't have a prayer. You're too far back." He exhaled a ring of smoke toward Arnold and chuckled.

Before I could even turn toward him, Arnold had kicked his chair back and stood from the table. "The hell I am," he snapped. He set his half-eaten burger back on the plate and brushed past our table without another word.

"Come on, let's go," Johnnie said, and we hustled off our seats and followed Arnold out of the lounge. He walked down a hallway and through a door with a sign over it that read *Men's Locker Room*. We did the same, but we both stopped when we saw Arnold sitting by his locker and retying his golf shoes. After making sure the laces were good and tight, he stood up and strode into the bathroom. Johnnie and I followed, and we saw him splashing water on his face and drying it with a towel. For several seconds, I watched Arnold Palmer glare at himself in the mirror. What did I see in that gaze? Determination? Grit?

I shook my head. No, those guesses were too easy to presume, and they were wrong. What I really saw was . . . *anger*. Whether he was mad at himself or with the sportswriter in the lounge, I couldn't tell, but Arnold Palmer's face was a deep red and his eyes seemed a tad bloodshot in the reflection from the glass. *Bulldog red* was what my father had called the look in a man's eyes when he was boiling mad. Arnold gave his face a rough rub with both hands and then turned on a dime. He headed toward me so fast, I couldn't get out of the way in time. I saw the whites of his eyeballs and heard the pounding of the man's heartbeat as he literally passed through me in one long glide. The sensation staggered me, and I felt Johnnie grip my forearm. I glanced down at the Scotsman. "He's really mad," I managed.

"Aye," Johnnie said. "Let's watch."

"Watch? What do you mean? The round is over."

Johnnie snorted. "This is 1960, lad. The third and fourth rounds were both played on Saturday. Our man there is about to start his fourth round."

I felt a surge of butterflies in my stomach as it dawned on me what I was about to witness. "Now?"

Johnnie's face broke into a wide grin. "Aye. In just a few minutes. Do you want to see him hit the shot?"

My eyes widened, knowing exactly the one he was talking about. I grinned back. "Aye."

28

THE FIRST HOLE AT CHERRY HILLS COUNTRY CLUB WAS A 346-yard downhill par four. Because of the slope and the higher altitudes in Colorado, the hole tempted golfers to go for the green off the tee. If they were able to pull off the shot, then they would have an eagle putt to start the day. Make it and they gained two shots on the field. Two-putt and they still had an easy birdie in hand to gain momentum.

It was the kind of shot my father would have called a fool's play. The fairway was tight and tree-lined on both sides, and there was water down the right side. Miss the shot and trouble lay everywhere. The quest to make an eagle or a two-putt birdie could easily become, in one bad swing, a test to save bogey or worse. I didn't need a history lesson to observe these challenges. Johnnie and I set up shop directly behind the tee box, and I was able to size up the hole in a matter of seconds.

"A fool's play," I whispered.

"Or a champion's," Johnnie fired back. When the Scotsman's temper flared, so did his accent, and the last word came out like "champeen."

"How did he fare on this hole the first three days?"

Johnnie shrugged. "Went for the green each time. Double bogey in round one after blocking his drive way right and into the creek. A scrambling par on day two after missing the green." Johnnie scratched his chin. "Missed the green again in round three and ended up three-putting for bogey."

I shook my head. "So, hitting driver off the tee had yielded a three-over total on one hole. That doesn't sound good."

"Mr. Clark," Johnnie began. "Perhaps it's not so much about pulling off the shot that counts, aye? Maybe it's believing that he can."

The words felt a bit like a punch to the gut, and I readjusted my feet on the grass. I glanced down at Johnnie, and he was looking right at me. His green eyes were fierce. "Have you ever thought about that?"

I didn't say anything, turning my attention back to the tee box and trying to ignore Johnnie's pointed question. A commotion had begun, and the patrons to the right of us were being told to make room. The one-thirty group was approaching.

I watched Arnold Palmer move through the gallery . . . his army . . . toward the tee box. It didn't appear that his short session on the driving range had done anything to quell his anger. As he stepped up onto the elevated mound where he would hit his first shot of the day, the agitation in his tense expression was obvious. Arnold snatched the driver out of his bag and tossed the cover to his caddy. Then he glared at the ground while his name was announced to the crowd: "And from Latrobe, Pennsylvania, Arnold Palmer." Unlike the times I had seen him as an elder statesman in practice rounds at Augusta, the look on the man's face now was all business. He barely watched as his playing partner struck what appeared to be a three wood down the left side of the fairway, well short of the green.

When it was his turn, Arnold teed his ball on the left-hand side of the marker. He stood behind the ball for a couple of seconds and gave his driver several soft swings with only his right hand. Then, without hesitation, he approached his ball and took his stance. He turned his head once to look at the target and, after returning his eyes to the ball, started his swing.

I had seen the golf swing of Arnold Palmer in his prime thousands of times on black-and-white videos, and I had watched the older version of the man hit live shots. It would be wrong to call his move on the ball a thing of beauty. He snatched the club back fast and made a full turn behind the ball, his clubhead dipping past the point where the shaft was parallel to the ground. Then he transitioned hard to his left side and lashed at the ball as if he were wielding a sword and literally trying to kill the white object on top of the tee. His follow-though was likewise violent as he stopped the clubhead out in front of him and cocked his head to the left. The move made him look like he was trying to will the ball to where he wanted it to go.

Was it beautiful? No. That was too weak a word. The man's swing was majestic and powerful. When Arnold's persimmon-headed club contacted the golf ball, the sound resembled that of a twelve-gauge shotgun.

I heard myself gasp at the sight and sound of the shot. Then I watched the ball take off on a dead line for the flag 346 yards away. The murmurs from the people around me turned into a rising quell of yells and then flat-out screams as the ball appeared to have a chance of reaching the green.

"He did it!" a man next to me hollered. I glanced at him and saw that he was holding binoculars tight to his eyes. "It's on the front of the green."

The man's voice was drowned out by more cheers from the

gallery as the news began to dawn on them all. When confirmation from the fans by the green had permeated back to the tee, the roar of excitement and joy from the army of patrons around me was stronger and louder than anything I'd ever heard in my life. Arnold Palmer had started the final round of the 1960 U.S. Open by driving the green on the par-four first hole. Through the shrill screams and applause, I heard voices of men, women, and children that seemed to come from every direction.

"Unbelievable!"

"Amazing!"

"He did it!"

"We love you, Arnold!"

"Yes!"

Arnold snatched his tee out of the ground and began to walk down the fairway. After a few feet, he hitched the back of his trousers, and I couldn't help but smile. When I did, I realized that my mouth had been hanging wide open. I had just seen one of the greatest shots in golf history. No telling of the Arnold Palmer legend was complete without mentioning him driving the green on the first hole at Cherry Hills in the final round of the U.S. Open.

And I had witnessed it.

As I took a step backward, I realized I was still squeezing my arms tight to my chest. I let out a deep breath. "He birdies this hole, right?" I was talking to myself as much as I was to Johnnie. "He birdies six out of the first seven, doesn't he?" I nodded to myself as the details came back to me. "Shoots his sixty-five, finishes at two eighty, and wins the tournament."

When I didn't hear any response from Johnnie, I looked

back for him, hoping that a return trip to the nineteenth hole might be in order. But he was gone. When my eyes returned to the tee box, it was gone too. The fairway in front of the tee was gone as well. As were all the people.

Everything . . . was gone.

29

I SAW NOTHING. JUST UTTER BLANKNESS.

No ground. No people. No vegetation. Complete nothingness.

What is happening?

I closed my eyes for a full three seconds. When I opened them, my head began to spin, and I reached back for something . . . anything to keep me from falling. My right hand clutched something soft and leathery. I looked at the material and tried to focus while I regained my balance.

It was a seat. A black leather seat. There was another one next to it and then a small window. I leaned forward and gazed out of the plexiglass, and my breath caught in my throat.

Blue skies. A few clouds. And, thousands of feet below, the outline of farmland. *I'm in an airplane.* I turned around and saw that the nothingness of a few seconds earlier had been replaced by the inside of a private jet. Turning toward the front of the plane, I saw a narrow opening that led to the cockpit. I took a tentative step forward and saw a pair of hands on the yoke.

Feeling my heart pounding in my chest, I continued forward. When I reached the opening, I saw a silver-haired man wearing a pink golf shirt and gray slacks behind the controls. He didn't look at me, but he didn't have to.

This was the Arnold Palmer with whom I was most familiar.

"What do you think of my jet?" he asked, and I heard the good-natured midwestern twang that had appeared in countless Hertz and Pennzoil commercials.

"It's nice," I managed. "Very impressive."

"Have a seat, Randy," he said, gesturing to the empty co-pilot's chair.

I hesitated for a moment, but then eased into the other seat in the cockpit.

"Did you know I was a pilot?"

I nodded, trying to find my voice. I cleared my throat. "There is a funny story of you flying the European Ryder Cup team around in your plane during one of the matches in the sixties."

Arnold laughed. "That was a lot of fun. Some good fellas on that Euro team."

"Some folks thought the Cup was over at that point," I said, trying to relax my nerves but not succeeding. I was sitting in the cockpit of Arnold Palmer's jet and talking to the King himself. "Because those guys were in awe of you."

Arnold shook his head, but the smile remained. "Sportswriter gobbledygook. We just played better than they did. The reporters always look for that dramatic angle, but the bottom line is usually a lot simpler."

I cocked my head at him. "You were Arnold Palmer. You had won a bunch of major championships. You had endorsement deals and were doing commercials. You could fly a jet airplane." I snorted. "You don't think those fellas were a little awestruck by you?"

He shrugged. "Maybe. Maybe not." He touched my forearm and then pointed at the yoke in front of me. "Take it."

"What?"

"Put your hands on the copilot's wheel."

"Why? I . . . I don't know how to fly a plane."

"Just do it, all right?"

I leaned forward and put my hands on the wheel. I glanced at Arnold, who had removed his own hands from the wheel in front of him.

He winked at me. "Now I want you to turn your wheel a little to the right and watch what happens out in front of this glass." He pointed toward the front windshield.

I did as I was told and noticed the nose of the airplane shift ever so slightly to the right. I couldn't help smiling as I gazed at the legend to my left. "I'm flying."

He punched my shoulder lightly. "You're flying. Now straighten her back up."

I took in a deep breath and slowly exhaled. Then I turned the wheel back to the left.

For the next ten minutes, Arnold Palmer, one of the greatest golfers to ever play the game and an icon in sport, gave me a lesson on how to fly an airplane. He explained the controls and what each of the different buttons did. He lectured on how to understand the coordinates and demonstrated how to maneuver the steering wheel to achieve what you wanted. When he finished his summation, I squinted at him. "How in the world did you find time to learn how to do this?"

"It meant something to me, so I made time."

"Why?" I asked, hearing the incredulity in my tone. "Why would you ever need to fly a plane?"

"I was scared of airplanes, Randy. Terrified of them. Afraid that I might die in a crash, and not all that crazy about heights. I learned how to fly so that I could conquer those fears." He paused. "It was the best thing I ever did."

"Oh, come on. You drove the green on the first hole of the U.S. Open and shot sixty-five to win. You played golf with presidents and royalty. You were the King of golf, for God's sake. How could learning to fly a plane be the best thing you ever did?"

He smiled and gazed out the front windshield. "I wasn't sure I could do it. I was afraid. But I pushed through my fear, believed in myself, trained and practiced hard with flight instructors, and"—he snapped his fingers—"I did it." He looked at me. "There's no greater feeling than overcoming a challenge that seems insurmountable."

I felt the same sense of being punched in the gut as I had on the tee box at Cherry Hills before watching Arnold hit his famous drive. Johnnie's words then came back to me. *Perhaps it's not so much about pulling off the shot that counts, aye? Maybe it's believing that he can.*

"You believed you could do it," I finally said. "Just like hitting driver off the first tee at Cherry Hills in 1960. You believed you could drive the green, and you eventually did it." I paused and looked at him. "You believed you could fly an airplane and overcome your fears, and you did it."

Arnold nodded, still gazing out the windshield. "That's true," he said. "But that's not all. Belief is very important, but it's only one part of the equation. You still have to practice and train hard." He finally turned his head to face me. "And then you have to do the most important thing." He paused. "The hardest thing."

I felt goose bumps rise on my arms as the intensity of his gaze fell over me. "What's that?"

"You have to go for it."

I raised my eyebrows, but Arnold Palmer's gaze remained trained on me as if he were sizing up a birdie putt. "You have to set your fears to the side and have the guts to go after what you want. Whether it's driving the first green at Cherry Hills or learning to fly an airplane, you eventually have to tee it up and let her rip."

"What if you crash?" I asked, hearing the timidity in my own voice. "What if you crash and lose everything?" I licked my lips and they felt dry as sandpaper. "What if you duck-hook your driver into the woods and make a double bogey?"

He punched my shoulder again, this time harder. The force behind the blow stung a little. "But what if you don't, Randy? What if you *win*?" He paused and turned back to the front of the plane. "You'll never overcome your fears and truly obtain victory unless you decide, once and for all, that you are going to pursue what you want with everything you have. That will mean taking a few risks, but that is a good thing. A life without risk is a life not lived." He paused. "Isn't it time you *lived*?"

I felt my heartbeat racing, and my hands were clammy with sweat. The airplane seemed to be moving faster. "What if I lose?"

"You may," Arnold said. "You may lose a lot. I sure as heck did. But you'll never *ever* win, unless you set aside the chains of doubt and fear . . . and go for it."

I couldn't think of anything to say and felt myself slinking down in the copilot's chair.

"Let me tell you something else, Randy." Arnold's voice

was quieter now. "The more you've lost. The harder you've been knocked down." He nodded to himself. "Those losses make the taste of victory that much sweeter." He paused, and his tone grew even softer, just more than a whisper. "But you'll never know, unless you pick yourself up off the ground and go after what you want."

30

I'M NOT SURE HOW LONG I SAT IN ARNOLD PALMER'S COPILOT seat. It was calm and peaceful up in the clouds thousands of feet above the ground. I gazed out the front windshield of that jet plane and images of my life began to flash in front of me. Playing Little League baseball and striking out the side to win the game. My dad, who coached the team, took us to Terry's Pizza to celebrate afterward and gave me the game ball. It was one of the happiest moments of my childhood. Moving forward to high school and seeing Mary Alice Davis for the first time in the hallway by the gym. It was the first day of fall football practice, and the cheerleaders were also practicing. Mary Alice was taking a sip of water from the fountain and some had dribbled down her chin. She turned and looked right at me and was oblivious to the droplets of moisture that ran down her chin and neck. Not me. I caught every single detail. Her blond hair, the long legs sprouting from her cheerleader's skirt, and the wondrous smile she gave me as she brushed past.

Then I saw that same smile on our wedding day. Mary

Alice at twenty-two in her wedding dress. I kissed her on the minister's cue.

As this memory faded, another less pleasant one took its place. I was gazing at a scoreboard with my hands stuffed in the pockets of my shorts. I felt a hand on my shoulder and a voice in my ear. "You'll make it next time, Randy. One measly stroke."

I knew that voice. It was Aubrey Wickenden, my teammate at Alabama. I had played number one on the team, and "Aubs," as we had called him, was number two. Aubs had gotten his tour card during Q school and I hadn't. My score had been better than his going into the final round, but he had closed with a sixty-eight and I had fired a seventy-four.

Then the scoreboard faded, and I was sitting in the kitchen of my parents' small home. My elbows were propped on the same table where my daughter, Davis, had eaten egg custard pie after Graham's funeral.

Now, I was at this table many years earlier, and Dad was breaking down why I should go to law school and forgo my dreams of the PGA Tour. "You've got a good woman, Randy. She's already agreed to work to help put you through school. Not every wife would be so supportive. She's pregnant, and you can't shirk your responsibilities and play the mini tours for another year in the hopes that Q school next year will work out different. Your mom and I can help you these next three years, and you can work during school yourself to make ends meet. When you graduate, you'll have something that I never had. You'll have a degree that will allow you to practice a profession." He had gazed down at his thick hands then. "Look at these, Randy." When I didn't look, he had grabbed my own hands and gripped them with his own, forcing me to meet his intense gaze. "Randy, all I've got is my ability to use my hands.

I'm a bricklayer, and I'm only as good as my last day's work." I had protested, arguing that he was more than that. That he owned his own company. That he had a crew of men who worked under him and who respected him.

But Dad had just chuckled and shaken his head. "They'd leave me in a half a second if I missed a day of work or if I didn't work harder than all of them. If you get a law degree, you'll have a job for the rest of your life. You'll have security that I could only have dreamed of."

I had slammed my fist down on the table and stood, turning my back on the man and the words I did not want to hear. "Dad, I missed the tour by one stroke."

"Son, you have a pregnant wife and it's time to stop chasing rainbows." Then he had paused and delivered the line that had stuck with me forever. "There comes a point in every man's life when he realizes that he's not going to be Joe Namath."

The image faded and was replaced by Coleman Coliseum in Tuscaloosa. My law school graduation. Dad shaking my hand on the gym floor with a proud look on his face, Mom kissing and then pinching my cheek, and Mary Alice holding two-year-old Davis in her arms. Had I been happy then? Proud? My three years of law school had been a blur of outlines and exams punctuated by summer clerkships in Birmingham and Huntsville and baby Davis's milestones. I had made it through and gotten my degree. A few months later, I had passed the bar exam and there was a similar scene on the steps of the capital in Montgomery, where the new inductees to the Alabama State Bar had taken a photograph.

Now, the images began picking up speed as if they were on fast forward. Funny how childhood and early-adult memories remained frozen in time and I could remember every detail, but my years of being a young attorney and father were a blur. The only pictures that were indelible were those of my children.

Davis's first steps in our small apartment in Tuscaloosa. Stumbling across the carpet with her arms held out, reaching for me and falling into my arms.

Our first Christmas in the new house on Locust, when Davis had stayed up all night waiting for Santa, finally passing out under the tree only to wake up and find the one present she'd asked him for leaning against the fireplace. Her first set of golf clubs. A woman's set with the shafts broken down so they'd fit her. The squeal that came out of her lungs when she opened her eyes that morning must have woken the neighbors.

Graham's birth at Huntsville Hospital. Holding my son for the first time and counting his fingers and toes, not realizing that I had tears in my eyes until my wife touched my face. Gazing at Mary Alice, whose face shone with radiance despite eight hours of labor. And then minutes later, introducing Davis, who was wearing a pink sweatshirt with *Big Sister* embroidered across the front, to her little brother.

And Davis's first golf tournament, the parent-child at Twickenham, where we'd finished second. The framed picture of us together, with Davis holding the tiny trophy and my arm around her, held a prominent place in our living room. Davis was ten years old, and her thick brown hair was tousled underneath a white visor. I could still remember our family's celebration dinner afterward at Boots' Steakhouse, where I shared the prime rib with my daughter, and she peppered me with questions about my time on the Alabama golf team and the mini tours and who I thought was better, Jack Nicklaus or Tom Watson. Mary Alice barely got a word in, but her face beamed with pride. We had all ordered blackberry cobbler for dessert, and

Graham, who was three and finally out of a high chair, got ice cream all over his T-shirt and pants.

Then the dark visions came. The pediatrician's office when the blood tests showed that Graham's white blood cell count was sky high. The awful nights when my son screamed and vomited from the pain and nausea of the radiation and chemo treatments. Last and worst of all, his death at the hospital.

And the emptiness that had followed. The hollow numbness of having lost someone whom I gladly would have died for. How many times had I wished it were me six feet under the ground and not my beautiful boy.

Tears began to stream down my face, and I brushed them away.

The sky was now dark in front of me. I turned to my left, but Arnold Palmer was gone. I had the same sense of blankness.

I took a deep breath and, remembering what I had done the last time, I closed my eyes and slowly counted to five. As I did, I thought about the last thing Arnold had said to me. *The more you've lost. The harder you've been knocked down . . . Those losses make the taste of victory that much sweeter. . . . But you'll never know, unless you pick yourself up off the ground and go after what you want.*

"What do I want?" I whispered, feeling a mixture of anxiety and adrenaline come over me as I slowly opened my eyes. I almost smiled as I took in the view that I had known best over the past decade.

I was gazing across my desk at the portrait of the thirteenth hole of Augusta.

"What do I want?" I repeated, speaking louder and hoping that Bobby Jones or Ben Hogan or Arnold Palmer or maybe even Johnnie would fire an answer back to me through the painting.

But the office was dead quiet.

I rose to my feet and walked around my desk to the portrait. I ran my index finger over the edges of the painted bunkers and, behind them, the azaleas. "What do I want?" I asked again for the third time.

I wasn't exactly sure, but I thought I knew the answer to another question. I knew what I didn't want.

I don't want to jump.

After thinking the words, I spoke them out loud. "I don't want to jump."

I took a tentative step back from the painting and sat on the edge of the desk. My hand felt something rough and I turned to see the crumpled-up note with Ellie Timberlake's request for lunch next week. I carefully straightened out the paper and placed it next to the telephone. I let out a deep breath and again peered at the painting across the room.

"What now, Darb?" Bobby Jones had taught self-control. Hogan had stood for resilience. And Arnold Palmer had shown with his words and actions the wisdom of believing in yourself and going after what you want.

But according to my dead friend, I still had one visit left. *Four rounds . . . four heroes . . .*

Could it be Jack? I wondered, grabbing my briefcase and walking out of the office. And if so, what would the Golden Bear have to tell me that the other three legends hadn't shared?

I smiled as I stepped outside and felt the sunshine on my face. For the first time in I couldn't remember when, I was excited about something.

FINAL ROUND

31

THAT NIGHT, WE DECIDED TO GO TO TERRY'S PIZZA AS A FAMily. Mary Alice was feeling better and wanted to eat something greasy, so we all split a large pepperoni, and Mary Alice and I both had draft Miller Lites while Davis washed her pizza down with a Dr Pepper. After taking my first bite of pie, I peered across the table at my daughter. "How'd the tourney go today, champ?" Davis hadn't said anything on the way to the restaurant, so I suspected she was disappointed in her play.

"Awful," she said, shaking her head as she chewed her food. "Shot eighty-nine and had thirty-seven putts. Couldn't make anything on the greens and quadruple-bogeyed the second hole."

I grimaced. "That one's a dogleg-right par five that goes up a hill and then down to the green, right?" I paused as she nodded. "The layup shot is tricky. Got to hug the left side and avoid going right."

Davis snorted. "Guess where I went?"

I took a sip of beer and grabbed her hand. "I'm sorry. I should have gone over the round with you beforehand like normal." I paused. "Won't happen again, okay?"

"Okay," she said, eyeing me warily. "But the quad on two

wasn't your fault. I was trying to go left with my layup and hit a cold shank." She made a swift left-to-right motion with her hand and sighed. "*Not* my best effort." Then she managed to laugh at herself.

I gripped her shoulder and chuckled in solidarity. The conversation turned to jokes about Bee Bee's cooking and discussion about the Masters, where Jack had fired a third-round sixty-nine and was now within four shots of the lead.

The leader at six under par was Greg Norman from Australia, whose linebacker build and flowing whitish-blond hair had earned him the nickname "the Great White Shark." Norman struck an intimidating figure on the course, and his aggressive style of play had made him one of the most popular players on tour. One shot behind the Shark at five under were Seve Ballesteros of Spain and Bernhard Langer from Germany, both former champions. Nick Price of South Africa was also five under, after tying the course record with a sixty-three. Two shots behind them were Tommy Nakajima of Japan and American stalwarts Tom Watson and Tom Kite.

Jack was two under, which put him within striking distance, but it was hard to imagine him coming from behind to beat the likes of Norman, Ballesteros, and Langer.

"At least he's got a chance," Davis said, sucking down some of her soda. "I'm betting he makes a charge."

I shook my head and winked at my wife, whose return smile wasn't as radiant as on our wedding day or by the water fountain in high school, but there was still some life in it. *When was the last time we had gone out for pizza as a family?*

I hadn't asked her about her day because I didn't want her to have to recall the trip to the cemetery. For her part, she hadn't asked me what I had done all day.

I chuckled to myself, wondering how I would even begin to describe what had happened at my office, and felt my wife's hand on top of mine. I looked across the table, which was covered with a checkerboard tablecloth, and her eyebrows were raised. "What are you laughing about?"

I shook my head. "Nothing."

"Tell me," she urged.

I glanced at Davis, who was also looking at me. "Spit it out, Dad."

"I'm still tickled by your mother's meat loaf."

"No, you're not," Mary Alice snapped. "I know you, Randy Clark, and something else is on your mind."

For a moment, I felt my stomach tighten. What in the world was I going to say? Then my litigation skills kicked in, and I talked myself out of the jam. "I went to the office, and I had a note to call Ellie Timberlake. She wants to have lunch and didn't say what it was about."

"Think she's going to offer you a job again?" Mary Alice asked. Her tone was noncommittal.

"I don't know. I doubt it. I suspect it has something to do with the circuit court judge spot that's opening up, but who knows?"

My wife nodded, but then she surprised me. Looking into her half-drunk beer mug, she spoke in a quiet voice. "If she does mention a partnership, you might want to consider it."

"I considered it last time, remember?"

She nodded, still gazing at the golden liquid in her glass. "Well . . . maybe the answer will be different this go-round." She glanced up from her glass with a tiny grin.

"Maybe," I said, smiling back at her.

32

I WOKE UP THE NEXT MORNING AT SIX O'CLOCK FEELING RE-freshed. I hadn't slept a full eight hours in years. Mercifully, there were no crazy dreams or nightmares.

I slipped on some tennis shoes, sweatpants, and a gray pull-over and decided to go for a run while Mary Alice and Davis were still snoozing. The morning air was cool, but the sun was rising, bringing warmth.

My joints were stiff at first, but after a few blocks they be-gan to loosen up. I hadn't been running in months, and the air felt good in my lungs. After a half a mile, I could sense the re-lease of endorphins in my body and mind.

The euphoria was short-lived. My knees began to ache and I developed a stitch in my side that required me to slow my pace to a brisk walk. That was fine, though, because I had reached my destination.

MAPLE HILL CEMETERY IS A ONE-HUNDRED-ACRE EXPANSE of land at the intersection of California Drive and McClung

Avenue. Once inside the gates, I walked at a steady pace toward my son's marker.

I wasn't sure why I needed to see him this morning, but I did. When I reached the Clark plot, I walked past the concrete slabs marking the graves of my grandfather and grandmother and my uncle Jack. Then I came to two markers side by side, shaded by a maple tree.

Robert Graham Clark. January 31, 1917—March 1, 1984

Robert Graham Clark II. February 14, 1978—March 3, 1983

My father . . . my son . . .

I leaned a hand against the maple. For a long time, I just stood there, focusing my eyes on my son's marker. Then I cleared my throat.

"We had a good time last night at Terry's, Graham. You would have loved it." I squatted down and ran my fingers over the letters of his name. "Your grandmother tried to kill your momma with her cooking again." I chuckled but felt the tears begin to slide down my cheeks. "Look, I . . . just wanted to say . . . that even though I don't come out here as much as your momma does, I really . . ." My words were choked out by a sob, and I let my knees fall to the ground. The grass was moist from the night's dew, and I felt the moisture soaking through my sweatpants.

I'm not sure how long I knelt by my son's grave and cried. I didn't think about the time. All I thought about was my boy and how much I loved and missed him. I cried for him and the unfairness of this cruel world. Finally, I gazed at the marker and finished what I had to say. "I love you, son, and I miss you so much. I thought that if I killed myself, it would make things better for everyone. That if I took my life, your sister could go to college and your momma could pay off our debts and hopefully find happiness with another man. A better man." I blinked back the tears. "And then the craziest thing happened." I smiled and looked up at the sky. "My friend Darby died." I let out a ragged laugh and shook my head. "And his ghost visited me. He told me I would be receiving a great gift and that I'd get to play a round of golf with four of my heroes." I snorted and rubbed my hand over my son's grave. "I told you it was crazy. I've played East Lake with Bobby Jones and learned about self-control. I've watched Ben Hogan hit perfect golf shots and learned about the incredible resilience he showed to get past his father's suicide and the bus crash that nearly crippled him. And I saw Arnold Palmer drive the green to win the 1960 U.S. Open. Arnold's lesson was to believe in yourself and go for what you want."

I stood up and brushed the wet grass off my pants. "And so now I'm not sure what I should do." I let out a deep breath and peered up at the sky. "But I'm not going to take my own life."

I peered down at the grave. "So, since my grand scheme to jump off the Tennessee River Bridge is out, I've got to figure out what to do and what I want."

I sighed and felt my lip beginning to tremble. When I spoke again, my voice was shaky. "I'm scared, son. For so long, I've felt stuck and overwhelmed. I think I want to move forward now, I really do." I closed my eyes. "I'm just not sure how."

I again knelt by the grave. "I love you, son. I wish it were me in there and you out here, but that's not the hand we were dealt. I hope I can make you proud of me. I hope . . ." Again, my voice shook. "We won't ever forget you, son, but I hope we can move forward with life. I know that's what we must do. I just . . . don't know how."

I kissed my hand and planted it over my son's name. Then I rose to my feet. For a long moment, I peered at the marker next to my son's, trying to speak without crying. "Take care of him up there, Dad." I wanted to say more, but I couldn't find the words.

33

I WALKED MOST OF THE WAY BACK HOME. I WAS TIRED FROM both the run and the emotions spent at the cemetery, but it was that good kind of fatigue that sets in after physical exertion. I knew I would feel better after a shower and some breakfast.

When I arrived at the house, Mary Alice's station wagon was gone. She'd left a note on the kitchen table. *Went to church with Davis. Love you.*

I felt the familiar pangs of remorse as I poured myself a glass of water and thought of my wife and daughter at church without me there. Before Graham's death, we had been regular attendees, but after burying our son, I had not had it in me to go back. Mary Alice and Davis had resumed going a few weeks after the funeral, but I had always found an excuse not to join them. Work, sickness, whatever. Finally, my wife had stopped asking me to come.

I sighed and drank the water in one long swig. I tried not to dwell on the guilt. Instead, I forced my legs to move toward the bathroom, where I started the shower running. As the hot water sprayed over my face and chest, I figured there was only one logical thing for me to do.

34

FORTY-FIVE MINUTES LATER, I PULLED INTO THE PARKING
lot of the Twickenham Country Club. As expected, my car was
one of only a handful in the lot. Most of the golf crowd, even
the scoundrels on the Big Team like Bland Simpson, were in
church right now. The course ought to be wide open.

There was one lesson left to go, and I wanted to get on with it.

I could feel my heart pounding in my chest. *Will I know
what to do after this one? Will I know how to move on?*

I set my bag on the driving range and walked down the hill
to the pro shop. On the way, I didn't see a soul. Though a light
crowd was common for Sunday, the emptiness of the place
seemed odd. There had been a few cars in the lot, so there had
to be some folks here. *Where are they?*

I opened the door to the pro shop, but there was no one behind the desk. I rang the bell on the counter and waited. Nothing. The lights in the back were off and there was no sign of life.
It's happening, I knew, feeling goose bumps come over my body.
The fourth and final round . . .

I stepped back outside and saw no one on the course or on

the path back to the range. However, as I walked up the hill, I saw a figure putting on the practice green. "Well, I'll be dipped in horse manure," I said out loud, laughing and picking up my pace. When I reached the green, I stopped and folded my arms across my chest.

"Nice putt," I said, as the other man rolled a ten-footer right into the heart of the hole.

"I make everything now," Darby said, rubbing his bushy beard. "Just like Ty Webb in *Caddyshack*."

"I thought you said you weren't my hero."

"I'm not," Darby said, stroking another putt, this time from twenty feet. When it curled into the side of the hole, he winked at me and shook his head.

"Then why are you here?"

"To say good-bye," Darby said, approaching me with his confident swagger. "And to wish you good luck."

"Why will I need luck?"

"Because the final lesson is the hardest, but also the most important." He sighed. "It's the one that I never learned."

"If you're not going to teach it, then who is?" I asked.

"Your real hero," Darby said.

"Jack?"

Darby smiled. "No. Jack Nicklaus is the greatest golfer that ever lived and a fine man." He paused. "But there is someone you look up to even more than Jack." Darby turned to the parking lot and pointed.

I squinted into the sun and saw a figure approaching. He was carrying a golf bag over his shoulder, and he looked to be in his late forties. When he got within ten feet of the practice green, I recognized him.

"Oh my God," I said.

35

HE LOOKED THE WAY I REMEMBERED HIM BEST. SALT-AND-pepper hair cut high and tight. Stocky build with massive, Popeye-like forearms. As he approached, he gave me a smile that showed the chipped front tooth he'd never gotten fixed. "Up for nine holes?" he asked, in the firm voice that, when it had been raised in anger, was the most terrifying sound in the world to me as a small boy.

I glanced to my left and saw that Darby was still standing beside me. "My dad?"

Darby nodded. "He won't recognize you unless you allow him to."

"How will I do that?" I asked.

But then Darby vanished as if he'd never been there at all. I blinked twice and looked again. Still gone. "Darb?"

"Hey." It was my father's voice.

I looked back toward him, and he was placing his bag by the first tee. "Did you hear me? Would you like to play nine?"

"S-S-Sure," I managed. I grabbed my bag and walked cautiously toward the first tee box. He had already set his bag on the ground and was taking out a few golf balls and tees from the front pouch.

I propped my bag up on its stand a few feet away from him.

He straightened himself and extended his hand. "My name is Robert Clark."

I shook my father's hand, and like when I was a kid, it felt like a brick that had been rubbed down with sandpaper. "R-R-Randy," I stuttered.

"That's my son's name."

"R-R-Really?"

"Yeah. Want me to toss a tee for the honors?"

"Okay."

He dug in his pocket and flung a white tee up in the air. When it landed, the tip was pointed more toward me than him. "You're up," he said, patting my back. Then he walked a few paces away and took two clubs out of his bag. He held them together and began to swing them; that was how he had always warmed up when we had played together.

"Want to hit a few on the range?" I asked, knowing what the response would be.

He chuckled. "And risk hitting a few good ones that I could've used on the course? I'll pass."

I laughed. That was exactly what he always said.

I snatched my driver out of the bag along with a ball and tee. *Is he going to recognize my swing?*

Darby's words drifted back to me. *He won't recognize you unless you allow him to . . .*

I shook off the thoughts as I stuck my tee in the ground and took a few practice swings. The first hole at Twickenham Country Club was a straightaway par four with a generous fairway. A nice, simple opening hole.

I addressed the ball and took my stance. Then, feeling oddly loose, I struck the ball pure. It launched off the tee down the left side of the fairway and then leaked toward the middle. It was the fade that I'd hit virtually my whole golf career.

"Nice one," my dad said, as he walked around me and teed up his own ball. I stood on the cart path and watched him take a quick peek at the fairway, address the ball, and then hit it with a short and choppy motion. The ball went fifty yards left of the fairway and then sliced back into the middle.

"That'll work," I said, smiling as I remembered that Dad had always just played his banana slice. He had never taken any golf lessons but managed to finagle the ball around the course and produce a decent score.

We walked down the fairway in silence, and I was reminded of all the rounds I'd played with my father over the years. So many of them had been like this. Both of us lost in our own thoughts. There had been a comfort in knowing that conversation was not expected. We were playing golf. If we had something to talk about, we would do so, but otherwise we were just . . . together.

I had taken the comfort I gained from playing with him for granted, but now, watching my father pounce down the fairway with his long stride and forward lean, I felt a warmth come over me. *This is . . . cool*, I thought. I was playing golf with my father as an equal.

Dad hit a fairway wood up close to the green for his second. Meanwhile, I flipped a wedge from 115 yards to within about a foot of the cup.

"Great shot!" Dad yelled as he passed by me.

"Thank you."

He chipped his ball to about five feet and, without taking a lot of time, made the putt for par.

I took a bit longer with my little putt. I found myself having those old feelings of wanting to please my father and not let him down by missing a gimme. I tried to shake them off, but it was no use. I snatched the putter head back too fast and decelerated coming through. Fortunately, the ball caught the side of the cup, curled around the hole, and finally landed inside it. I sighed and snatched the ball out of the cup. Then I glanced over at him, and he was grinning at me.

"Nice birdie," he said, but I could tell by his wry expression that he thought I'd gotten lucky.

"Almost choked it," I said, feeling like the fifteen-year-old version of myself and unable to meet his eye.

He didn't say anything as we walked side by side to the next hole. "What do you do for a living?" Dad asked, as I put my tee in the ground on the second tee box.

"I'm a lawyer," I said. "Personal-injury defense work."

Dad smiled, but there was a sadness in his eyes. "I would love for my son to get in that kind of career."

I saw an opportunity. "How old is your son?"

"Twenty-four."

Without thinking much about my shot, I stepped into my stance and drilled a nice drive down the right side of the fairway. The second hole at Twickenham was a 515-yard par five and, but for a big oak tree that could block you if you went too far to the right, had no trouble except for a creek that guarded the front of the green.

"Good shot," Dad said. As he put his tee in the ground, he grunted and said, "My boy wants to be a professional golfer."

Before I could respond, Dad hit his typical banana slice. This time, his shot sliced too much and ended up behind the tree on the right.

"Do you think he can make the tour?" I asked, as we walked toward our respective shots.

"Yes," Dad said, and I felt my heart flutter at his lack of hesitation. "I know he can."

I was dumbfounded by what I had heard and had to compose myself to be able to respond. After several more strides, I cleared my throat and tried to keep him going. "Well . . . that's good, isn't it? If that's what he wants to do?"

"I don't know," Dad said, beginning to veer toward the right where his ball was blocked by the oak tree. "At what cost, you know?" He ambled away, and I knew it would be awkward if I followed him. Without taking more than fifteen seconds to size up his shot, he punched a ball under the tree branches, and it rolled down the fairway to one hundred yards from the green. It was an incredible shot, but Dad acted like he'd hit it a hundred times.

He probably has, I thought, remembering all the knockdown shots I'd seen Dad hit out of the trouble that his slice off the tee put him in. I turned my attention to my shot. I was 220 yards from the green. This was a good distance for me, because I knew I could carry a three wood to the front fringe, and it ought to roll out to pin high. *If I hit it solid . . .*

Without allowing myself to think about it too much, I took out the three wood and addressed my ball. I hit it as pure as snow.

The ball started off left of the flag, turned slightly right, and landed on the front of the green. When it finished rolling, it appeared that I'd have about fifteen feet for eagle.

"Looks like you're the one that ought to be on the tour," Dad said, as our paths connected again.

"Lucky shot."

"I know better than that," Dad snorted. "Your swing reminds me of my boy Randy's. The power fade. That's what Hogan and Nicklaus hit, and they were the straightest drivers in the game."

I felt heat on my face and knew I was blushing. "I don't hit it as far as those guys."

"Neither does my son. One thing that's holding him back is his distance, but I still think he can make it based on the overall strength of his game."

"You don't sound very happy about it."

He shrugged. "Like I was saying. At what cost? He's married to a sweet gal, and she's pregnant." He smiled. "Gonna have my first grandchild." Now, it was his face that was beaming.

"Congratulations."

"Thanks." He stopped at his ball and grabbed a wedge out of his tote bag. Without taking a practice swing, he addressed his ball, took one look at the green, and swung.

The ball landed about ten feet left of the flag and spun to the right. I doubted he had more than a five-footer left for birdie. I smiled and shook my head. "You sure don't take much time."

"What's the point?" Dad asked, reshouldering his bag after putting the wedge inside. "My lick isn't going to get any better with practice swings, and I know where I want to hit it."

I chuckled. "I see your point. So, you were talking about the cost of being a pro golfer. You think it's too much?"

Dad gave his head a jerk. "The time. The money. The travel. That's going to be hard on a young family. There's also the lack of any assurance or guarantee that he'll be successful. There's no job security."

"Well . . ." I thought of what Arnold Palmer had told me in his airplane. "Sometimes, don't you have to believe in yourself enough to take a few risks?"

He looked at me with his steel-blue eyes, and just like that, I felt like I was twelve years old again in the backyard and he was showing me a patch of grass I'd failed to get with the mower. "That's not a luxury that a young father has. I've spent my whole life working with my hands. I'm only as good as how well I can use them, and being a professional golfer is no different. Sure, if he's really successful, then he might make more money, but the minute he stops making putts or if he loses his confidence, then there goes his career. Poof in the wind, and he's got nothing." Dad marked his ball and again peered at me with those piercing eyes that were as cold as ice. "I want more for my boy than a life that depends on how well he can use his hands. I want the same for my grandson or granddaughter, whatever the case may be."

I marked my ball. "Have you told your son that?"

"I've tried to." Then he let out a long sigh. "You got kids?"

"Yeah. I have a teenage daughter."

"Have you ever tried to tell her something and had it come out wrong?"

I smiled. I had never had a conversation like this with my father. I had never heard him admit that he had difficulty talking to me. "Many times," I finally said. Then, seeing the frustration in Dad's eyes, I added, "It's not easy being a father."

He peered at me for several seconds, and for a brief moment, my stomach tightened. *Does he recognize me?*

Then, gesturing toward the hole with his putter, he said. "I'd kind of like to see an eagle."

36

I MISSED THE PUTT FOR EAGLE BUT LEFT MYSELF AN EASY tap-in for birdie. Dad lipped his birdie putt out and settled for par. We walked to the next hole, and I hoped that we might continue our conversation about his son. *Me* . . .

But alas, Dad went back into silent mode. It was his way, and I wasn't surprised. Dad had never been a talker, and I suspected he felt that he'd already said too much. Other than a few "good shots" here and there, the next six holes were spent playing golf and doing little else. Despite the lack of conversation, I had to admit that I was enjoying myself. I was also four under par, adding two more birdies. For his part, Dad had scrounged around in three over, making no worse than bogey but unable to give himself any more birdie looks.

The eighth hole at Twickenham was a two-hundred-yard par three with out of bounds to the left and bunkers and tree trouble to the right. It was a tough hole that required a well-executed long iron. I grabbed my three iron and struck the ball solid. It rose high into the air and landed ten feet to the left of the flag.

"Beautiful shot," Dad said. "You're a heck of a golfer, Randy."

"Thank you, D-D . . ." I stopped myself before I said the word. "Thank you, Robert."

He again peered at me for several seconds. "You look awful familiar," he finally said.

"You do too."

He struck his shot, and the ball sliced into the sand trap that guarded the right side of the green. As we walked toward the green, I realized I was running out of time and there was something else I wanted to ask him. "Robert, when you tried to explain the costs of being a PGA Tour golfer to your son, you said it came out wrong. How do you mean?"

"Why do you want to know?"

I felt my stomach clench. *Because I'm your son and I've wanted to know this my whole life* . . . I sucked in a quick breath and chose my words carefully. "Because I'm a father, and I'm having my own problems communicating with my daughter."

"I used an analogy. I told him that there comes a time in every man's life when he realizes he isn't going to be Joe Namath."

I felt gooseflesh rise on my forearms, as I heard him repeat the words that had been the bumper sticker of my life for the past sixteen years.

"I felt the meaning was obvious. Joe Namath was the most famous athlete in the world at one time. He was Broadway Joe. That type of fame comes with a price, and I think every man who has the responsibilities of a husband and father, at some point, realizes that he can't live that life anymore." He sighed. "But I guess I was also saying something else."

"You were telling him he wasn't good enough." The words burned coming out of my mouth, and they sounded harsh and unsympathetic. Dad's shoulders sagged but he didn't say anything. "You were telling him that he didn't have the talent and skill to be a pro golfer and that he should give up that pipe dream to do something more practical."

Dad stopped by the bunker and took out his sand wedge. For a long moment, he paused, looking at the ground. "That's right," he finally said.

"But you told me earlier that you did think he was good enough to make it. Why would you tell your son something different?"

Dad continued to peer at the grass. "I don't know. My son had a friend who had made the tour." He gave his head another jerk. "A scalawag named Darby Hays that I knew was bad news, but Randy was blind to that. He worshipped Darby because he had made the tour and was playing with Arnold and Jack. Randy could never see past getting his tour card. He couldn't picture the life he'd be living away from his wife and child." He paused. "Was he good enough to make it? Yes, he was. Was he good enough to win on tour?" He sighed. "I don't know."

"Why wouldn't you want your son to chase his dream?" I asked. "What would have been the harm in that?"

Dad finally peered up at me. "I was trying to be a good father and give sound advice." He paused. "I was wrong, and I'll never forgive myself."

I felt the air go out of my lungs, and my arms hung limp at my sides. I couldn't believe what I'd just heard. Then I asked another question. "Why can't you forgive yourself?"

"Because I'm not sure my boy is ever going to believe in himself again. He's in law school now and making good grades, but there's something missing. Something I took from him."

"What?"

My father gazed at me and his blue eyes were no longer cold. They were sad and tormented. "His spirit."

I FINISHED OUT THE EIGHTH HOLE IN A DAZE, TRYING TO come to grips with what my father had admitted. *All these years,* I thought. *All that time.* I was angry that Dad had never told me he had been wrong. *Why couldn't he have taken it back?*

But how do you tell your son that he is good enough when you've already informed him that he isn't?

More than anger, though, the primary emotion permeating my being was sadness. For my father. For me. For us.

The ninth hole at Twickenham was an uphill par four that ran adjacent to the first hole on the right and Airport Road on the left. As we hit our tee shots, the sounds of cars passing by could be heard. Dad sliced his drive all the way into the first fairway, while I blocked my ball in the same direction.

"Not our best," I said, as we trudged off the tee box.

"Nope."

We both ended up hitting low punch shots for our approaches. Mine finished in the front bunker, but Dad hit a perfect run-up shot that finished on the front portion of the green.

As we walked, I noticed that the sun was beginning to drop, which didn't make sense. It couldn't be more than two o'clock in the afternoon.

Does anything make sense in these dreams?

By the time we reached the green, the sunlight had faded, and dusk was upon us. I hit a sand shot that finished a couple inches from the hole.

"That's good," Dad said.

I picked my ball up and began to feel heat behind my eyes. The round was almost over. How much more time did I have with my father?"

I took out the pin and looked at the man that I had worshipped since I was old enough to think. Dad thought my hero was Darby Hays, and I guess maybe I had thought that at one time too.

No. I knew, feeling the tears begin to fall down my cheeks. *I'm looking at my hero right now.* He peered at the hole and crouched over the putt with a pigeon-toed stance reminiscent of Arnold Palmer. He struck the putt and then watched the ball keenly as it made its way toward the hole. Instead of following the ball, I looked at Dad. His Popeye-like arms. The chest hair that poked out of his golf shirt. The salt-and-pepper hair. Had I ever known him when he didn't have gray in his hair? I remembered the smell of his aftershave when I used to sit in his lap on Christmas Eve while he read " 'Twas the Night before Christmas."

I heard the ball land in the cup and then looked down and saw the evidence. I smiled and wiped my eyes. Then I knelt down and retrieved his ball, flipping it to him and putting the flagstick back in the hole. "Nice birdie."

"Better late than never."

For a few seconds, we gazed at each other, and then he extended his hand. "Well, Randy, I really enjoyed that. Maybe we can play again some time."

I held on to his firm hand and couldn't find my tongue. All I could do was nod.

He started to walk away, and I watched him, feeling my heartbeat racing.

He won't recognize you unless you allow him to . . .

Finally, as he reached the fringe of the green and was placing his putter in his bag, I found my voice.

"Hey, Dad."

He looked up from his golf bag and squinted at me. Behind him, I saw the sun setting orange on the western horizon. Then, slowly, he walked back toward me. When he was a foot away, I noticed that his salt-and-pepper hair had turned completely salt and he had aged another twenty years.

"Son," he said. He smiled but it appeared forced. "That was quite a round you fired. Four under by my count."

"Thank you."

For another few seconds, we gazed at each other. The sun had almost completely disappeared, and I knew that my journey that had started with a visit from the ghost of Darby Hays had come to an end. It had all led up to this moment.

This is the most important lesson . . .

"Dad, can you do something for me?"

He nodded.

"I need you to forgive yourself."

"Why?" he asked. "I broke your spirit. You were never the same. What I did . . . was unforgivable."

"No," I said. "I . . . forgive you." I nodded as I said the words and then, because it felt good coming out of my mouth,

I said them louder. "I forgive you, Dad. You were trying to be a good father, and I forgive you."

For the first time in my life, I saw tears in my father's eyes. "What about Graham? You were in the worst storm of your life, and I died on you right after Graham. You needed me, and I failed you."

"No, you didn't," I said, hearing the truth in my own tone. "No, Dad, it was you who gave me the strength to get through Graham's passing. You were a tough and demanding father. You taught me to take care of my family first. To be responsible." I paused. "You taught me how to be a man, and I relied on every one of those lessons during Graham's illness and death."

He wiped the tears from his face. It was so dark now that all I could see was his shadow and his blue eyes peering back at me. "Randy, you're the strongest man I've ever known." The words resembled what I'd heard him tell Davis on the day of Graham's funeral.

I extended my hand, and he took it. Then we hugged, and I smelled the familiar aftershave that would always remind me of Christmas Eve. "I love you, Dad."

"I love you too, son."

We unlocked our embrace, and he began to walk away. After a few steps, I could barely see him.

"Dad?"

"Randy, there's one more thing you need to do."

"What?"

"Forgive yourself. Let go of the failures. Of the self-doubt. Of the grief over Graham. Of everything you've been beating yourself up over." He paused. "Set it all down on this green . . . and forgive yourself."

38

I'M NOT SURE HOW LONG I STOOD ON THE GREEN OF THE ninth hole of Twickenham Country Club. It could have been thirty minutes. It could have been three hours. I lost all track of time. Eventually, I sat down on the damp dew-stained grass, crossed my legs, and bowed my head.

And I cried.

I prayed and asked God to forgive my sins.

I cried some more.

And then, somewhere in the darkness, I took my father's final advice. I closed my eyes and spoke the words out loud.

"I forgive you, Randy. You've made mistakes. You've failed. I forgive you."

I forgive you.

I forgive you.

I took a deep breath and exhaled.

I forgive me.

39

WHEN I OPENED MY EYES, I WAS SITTING BEHIND THE WHEEL of my car. Fierce light shone through the front window, and I had to shield my face from the glare.

I glanced at the clock on the dash. It was three in the afternoon. *How long have I been sitting here?* I looked around the parking lot, and it was almost as empty as it had been when I arrived over five hours ago.

Masters Sunday, I thought. Everyone was probably at home glued to their television sets, watching Greg Norman and Seve Ballesteros battle it out for world golf supremacy.

I took a deep breath and whispered the last thing I could remember about my round with Dad. "I forgive me."

Then I smiled. I noticed that my keys were in the ignition, and I cranked the car to life. I pulled out of the parking lot, going over everything I had learned over the past four days.

Self-control . . . In order to stop beating yourself, you have to learn and practice self-control.

Resilience . . . Be resilient in the face of great adversity.

Belief . . . Believe in yourself and go after what you want.

Forgiveness . . . Forgive the people who have caused you the most hurt. In my case, my dad . . . and myself.

I drove home on autopilot, remembering the smoothness with which Bobby Jones had swung the golf club and the haunting eyes of young Bobby in his hotel room in Scotland before he had gained control of himself. I thought of nine-year-old Ben Hogan, following his father into his parents' bedroom and watching Chester Hogan shoot himself. Next I saw Arnold Palmer, smashing his opening drive toward the first green at Cherry Hills and charging electricity though the crowd with the boldness of his play and then sitting in the cockpit of his jet. Finally, I remembered my father's blue eyes.

As I pulled into the driveway, I thought about the Masters. It was the final round, and everyone knew that the Masters didn't really start until the back nine on Sunday. *Which the leaders should be playing right about now* . . .

I parked behind Mary Alice's station wagon and sighed, hoping that my wife wouldn't be mad at me for essentially disappearing for six hours. But as I walked toward the front door, I was greeted by a surprise. The door shot open, and Davis gazed at me wild-eyed. "Dad, where have you been?" Her voice was breathless, and I saw sweat beads on her forehead.

"At the club. Why? What's the matter?"

"Randy, you need to come in here right now." It was Mary Alice. She sounded almost giddy.

"Dad." A smile lit up my daughter's face. "You're not going to believe it."

NINETEENTH HOLE

40

ON SUNDAY, APRIL 13, 1986, ON AN ABSOLUTELY GORGEOUS spring day in Augusta, Georgia, Jack William Nicklaus won the Masters.

I got home in time to watch Jack's final four holes with my wife and daughter. Davis was so nervous that she did push-ups and jumping jacks in between shots. That was why she was sweating. Mary Alice, who had never showed a lot of emotion during a golf tournament, squeezed my hand tight and pulled for Jack as if her life depended on it. We were seeing something that shouldn't happen. A forty-six-year-old man should not win the Masters.

But yet, there he was, the Golden Bear, dressed in a yellow golf shirt and plaid pants, stalking down the fifteenth hole after a huge drive and chasing Ballesteros and Norman. I'll never forget the feeling of watching Jack's second shot on fifteen. It was the first action of the tournament I got to see. The fifteenth hole is a breathtaking par five with water in front of the green and behind it. If a player hits a good drive, as Jack had done, then he can go for the green in two shots, setting up a chance for eagle. As Jack took his stance, I held my breath and heard not a sound, either on the television or in our small den. In the distance, I saw the green and then Jack took his stance. Even on TV, I could tell by the sound of the club hitting the ball that he had caught it pure. And then, like a bear stalking his prey, Jack Nicklaus walked after the ball, as if he were willing it to go exactly where he wanted it.

The ball landed just to the left of the flag and finished about twelve feet away. On the television, announcer Ben Wright screamed in his English accent, "He's got a chance! He's got a very good chance!"

I felt adrenaline tingle through my body, and my wife's hand gripped my own in a death squeeze. I looked at her, and Mary Alice was radiant.

"He's got a chance." She repeated the broadcaster's words, even mimicking the English inflection.

"Since when do you care about golf?" I asked.

"Since my husband's favorite player decided to make a charge in the final round of the Masters."

An image of my father's fist pump from when Jack made the forty-foot snake on the sixteenth hole in 1975 popped into my mind. *Is this really happening?*

Minutes later, Jack made his eagle putt to climb within two of the lead. On the sixteenth tee box, there was a long wait, as often is the case with par-three holes. The sixteenth was a par three over water and had provided a lot of drama in years past in the tournament. As Jack prepared to address the ball, the loud roars gave way to stone silence. Again, even on the television screen, Jack's shot sounded solid. After hitting the ball, Jack immediately bent down to get his tee, not even looking at the hole.

Seconds later, the ball landed three feet to the right of the hole and then began to spin.

"It's going to go in!" Davis screamed.

But the ball grazed the edge of the cup, leaving a straight uphill putt for birdie. When Jack made that putt, it sounded like a rock concert had broken out at Augusta. One shot back.

As Jack played the seventeenth hole, Seve Ballesteros, still in the lead, was hitting his second shot to the par-five fifteenth. I didn't want to root against another player, but I knew that if Seve hit the green, he'd probably make at worst case a birdie. Again, I held my breath. When the Spaniard made contact, I could tell he didn't like it almost immediately. The ball hooked on a low line and landed in the pond fronting the fifteenth green.

"Unbelievable," I whispered, looking at Davis, who was covering the sides of her face with both hands and gaping at the television set. Ballesteros went from an easy birdie to having to scramble to make bogey, which he was able to do. Still, with two holes left to play, Jack Nicklaus was tied for the lead.

Jack hit a so-so drive on seventeen that left him with a shot between two trees. He hit the recovery shot well, though, and was able to find the green, about ten feet from the cup. As he addressed his ball, announcer Verne Lundquist whispered what the putt would mean. "This is for sole possession of the lead."

Below me, Davis had stopped doing push-ups and had wrapped her arms around her knees. Mary Alice had sat down on the couch and clasped her hands together in front of her mouth. I took a deep breath and began to have a hard time controlling my emotions. Here was a person in full possession of all the attributes I had been taught these last few days. Jack was in total self-control. He had fought bravely to put himself in position to win a major championship at forty-six years old, enduring the wisecracks that his clubs were rusty and the quips about his huge putter blade. He had faced that adversity down and pushed through it. The man radiated confidence and believed in his own abilities and here he was, going for it. I'd also heard the announcers mention a bogey that he'd made on the twelfth hole that could have derailed Jack's round, but he had forgiven himself for that mistake and pushed forward.

Jack struck the putt, and as the ball was halfway there, it looked like it was going to miss to the right. And then Jack stepped toward the ball and began to raise his putter with his left hand. The ball remarkably held straight, and Lundquist said, "Maybe . . ."

When the ball found the bottom of the cup, the announcer yelled, "Yes, sir!"

As Jack played the eighteenth hole, I sat beside my wife on the couch and put my arm around her. As I breathed in the familiar scent of her perfume, I began to cry. I thought of what I had almost done a few days before. A vision of the river from the Tennessee River Bridge came into my mind, and a tear formed. *If Darby Hays hadn't come to see me . . .*

"Randy, are you okay?"

I wiped my eyes and smiled at her.

"Dad?" Davis had begun doing push-ups again but had stopped when she heard her mother's question.

"I'm fine. I'm just . . . happy." I nodded as I said a word I hadn't uttered in a very long time. I wrinkled my face in an effort to stop the tears. Then, as if to confirm my feelings, I said it again. "Happy."

Jack made par on the eighteenth hole. After sinking his final putt, he hugged his son Jackie, and they walked off the green together. By this point, Mary Alice and I were both crying, and Davis was also wiping her eyes. It was the most perfect sports moment I had ever seen.

Thirty minutes later, Greg Norman's late charge ended with a bogey on the last hole, and Jack had done it. He'd won the Masters for the sixth time.

MARY ALICE, DAVIS, AND I WERE QUIET DURING THE POST-tournament ceremony, where the chairman of Augusta National Golf Club presented the green jacket to Jack Nicklaus. Given what I'd experienced in the last four days, ending with such an emotional tournament, I was exhausted, and it seemed that my daughter and wife were also drained.

But as the prior year's champion placed the coat around Jack's shoulders, I knew there was something I had to do. I rested my hand on my wife's knee and leaned toward her. "I'm sorry," I whispered.

"For what?" she asked, gazing up at me.

"For checking out after Graham's death. For not being stronger." I paused. "For everything. Can you forgive me?"

Her lip trembled and she nodded. Then, moving closer, she wrapped her arms around me and kissed my cheek. "I love you, Randy," she said, her voice soft, her breath warm on my ear.

"I love you too."

I started to pull away, but she held tight to my shoulders. "Maybe tonight," she said, "after Davis goes to bed, we can . . . you know . . ."

"What?" I asked, not getting it immediately. I looked into her brown eyes and she smiled.

"It's been a long time," she said.

"Too long," I agreed. Then I leaned in and planted a kiss on her lips.

"You guys need a room?" Davis asked in her patented sarcastic teenager voice that couldn't quite hide her smile.

"Maybe," Mary Alice said.

"Mom!" Davis yelled.

I began to chuckle and then, seeing that Mary Alice had also gotten tickled, I laughed long and hard. So hard that my sides began to hurt.

When the giggling fit had finally subsided, I moved my eyes from my wife to my daughter and took in a deep breath. As I slowly exhaled, I couldn't believe my good fortune.

I was not dead and no longer wanted to be. I was alive and grateful for my life, as messy as it was.

Thank you, Darb, I thought, and then I bowed my head. *Thank you, God.*

I wasn't Joe Namath and I never would be. I was Randall James Clark. I wiped the tears out of my eyes and looked up at my daughter and wife.

And I'm okay with that.

41

FOURTEEN MONTHS AFTER JACK NICKLAUS WON HIS SIXTH green jacket, I stood on the first tee of Turtle Point Country Club in Killen, Alabama. I had butterflies in my stomach and had barely touched my bowl of cereal at the hotel breakfast bar that morning. I pulled the three wood out of the bag and ran my fingers along the Golf Pride grip that I had installed last week. It felt tacky and good in my hands. Then I looked up and watched the player on the tee. Her name was Briana Proud, and her long, fluid swing and thick black hair reminded me of LPGA legend Nancy Lopez. This would be the third day that we'd played with her, and she was leading the tournament by two shots.

As Proud sized up her shot from behind the ball, I leaned forward and whispered, "Just like yesterday. Hit the ball solid. Play our draw. That should put us on the left side of the fairway with a wedge." Then I patted my daughter on the back and gave her neck a squeeze. "Regardless of what happens, I'm proud of you. The Southern Junior Amateur is a hard tournament to qualify for, much less have a chance to win."

Davis looked up at me with her grandfather's blue eyes. She wore a white cap and her ponytail stuck out of the opening in the back of it. She'd grown a good four inches in the last year, and her tall, skinny frame produced a smooth and powerful golf swing. "I'm five shots back, and I'm not as good as this girl, Dad. She's beaten me each day we've played with her."

I gave her neck another tug. "It's not your job to beat her. You be you and play the best you can play. Focus on your game and keep your mind calm."

"Self-control," she whispered. It was a mantra we had developed during my caddying for her this summer.

"Stay in control of your emotions and don't beat yourself," I uttered my part.

"Resilience," she said, her voice quiet and firm.

"Face adversity head on and don't run from it."

"Believe in myself and take risks."

"Go for it," I said.

She smiled. "Go for it." Then, the grin gone, she added, "Forgive my mistakes."

"Set them down and move on."

For a moment, we stopped our quiet chatter as Proud addressed the ball. She waggled her club, stared down the target, and then launched a high cut with what looked like a five wood down the left side of the fairway.

"Nice shot," Davis and I both said at the same time.

Davis looked at me, and I handed her the three wood. "Good luck, champ."

She took the club but held on to my hand. "Dad?"

"Yeah."

"I'm proud of you too."

I cocked my head at her.

"I mean it," she continued. "Our family was on the verge of falling apart last year, but you saved us."

I smiled. "I had a lot of help from Ellie Timberlake. If she hadn't offered me another chance at a partnership and we hadn't had those two big settlements before the end of the year . . ."

"That was risky going with Ms. Ellie after being with the firm for so long," she said. "You put everything you've been teaching me this summer into practice, and you did it."

"I had a lot of support from you and your momma." I paused, thinking back to Christmas Eve, when I'd snuck up behind Mary Alice and Davis while they were wrapping presents in front of the tree and held the release from the hospital in front of my wife's angelic face. "It's over," I whispered in her ear.

Mary Alice had read the first few words of the document and then her chest began to heave. She looked at me, her eyes glistening. "You did it," she said.

"We did it," I corrected, hugging her tight. That night, my mother had brought over her famous egg custard pie, which did indeed make everything better, and we'd celebrated in style. I even read " 'Twas the Night before Christmas," hoping that my daughter might one day think of me when she read this story to her own kids as I thought of my own father.

Davis squeezed my hand, bringing me back to the present. Then she let go and took a couple of steps backward, still gazing at me, her face breaking into a mischievous smile. "You think any more about what I mentioned last night?"

I smirked at her. "Just hit the ball, will you?"

But she continued to gaze at me. "Senior tour, baby. You'll be fifty in what, nine years? Maybe we'll both be pro golfers then."

I shook my head and pointed at the fairway. "Hit."

She laughed, and the sound warmed my heart. Then she turned and placed her tee in the ground. While she sized up her shot, I tingled with pride, love, and something else perhaps even more powerful.

Gratitude.

In the months since I'd received the four lessons bestowed upon me by the ghosts of Bobby Jones, Ben Hogan, Arnold Palmer, and my father, I had added a fifth that I thought might be equal in importance.

I was grateful.

For the gift of life and all its mysteries, challenges, and wonders.

For my wife, Mary Alice, my best friend and soulmate.

For my daughter, Davis, who was becoming a woman before my eyes.

For my son, Graham, whom we lost to cancer but not before he left us so many precious memories.

For my mother, whose unconditional love was something I'd never take for granted again.

For my father, whose words burned my soul but whose love, support, and toughness made me the man I am.

And for God, in whom I have a renewed faith. How else could I ever explain the miracle that was given to me?

Four heroes . . . Four rounds . . . Four lessons . . .

"Thank you," I whispered, as my daughter hit her first tee shot.

Thank you.

AUTHOR'S NOTE

After his family, my father's greatest passion was the game of golf, and his hero was "the Golden Bear," Jack Nicklaus. During the final round of the 1986 Masters, when Jack charged up the leaderboard, Dad became so nervous that he left the house to mow the grass. After Jack hit his approach close on the fifteenth hole, I made Dad come inside for the conclusion. The first time I ever cried watching a sporting event was when Jack hugged his son Jackie after finishing the winning round. Echoing Randy Clark at the end of this book, it was the most perfect sports moment I had ever seen and would remain so until Tiger Woods's victory at Augusta in April 2019.

In the summer of 2015, Dad, my brother Bo, and I played East Lake Golf Club in Atlanta, Georgia. As you know from reading this story, East Lake was the home course of Bobby Jones. This was to be the first of four excursions. We would play Scioto in Ohio, Jack's home course; Shady Oaks Country Club in Fort Worth, Texas, the course Ben Hogan founded; and Latrobe Country Club in Latrobe, Pennsylvania, where Arnold Palmer's father was once the pro and the course where the King learned the game.

Dad wanted one last golf odyssey with his sons at the

courses sacred to the players on his Mount Rushmore: Jones, Hogan, Palmer, and Nicklaus. As we drove home from Atlanta, I thought that perhaps I should write a memoir about our adventures, but as it turned out, East Lake would be the only leg of the journey we were able to complete.

In April 2016, Dad was diagnosed with stage-four lung cancer. Eight months later, my wife, Dixie, was diagnosed with early stage-three lung cancer. Dad died on March 3, 2017. Thirty days later, exactly a month after Dad's death, Dixie had curative surgery to remove most of her right lung. In the aftermath, I began to think about turning Dad's unfulfilled dream into a fable that might help people during hard times and offer a glimmer of hope in the darkness of life.

Four heroes . . . Four rounds . . . Four lessons.

Thank you for reading *The Golfer's Carol*. As I finish this voyage, I am grateful for the story of Randy Clark, whom I named after my hero.

My dad, Randy Bailey.

ROBERT BAILEY
DECEMBER 9, 2019

ACKNOWLEDGMENTS

My wife, Dixie, has been there on this journey since the first word. I'm so thankful for her presence, her health, and her love. She is my everything.

Our children—Jimmy, Bobby, and Allie—inspire me every day.

My mother, Beth Bailey, is always my first reader, and her questions, ideas, and support mean more to me than words can say.

My agent, Liza Fleissig, has helped me achieve my dreams. I am forever grateful for Liza's efforts and persistence.

Thank you to Tara Singh Carlson, my editor, for her expertise, passion, and vision. Also, special thanks to Helen O'Hare for her assistance on this book and all of the great folks at G. P. Putnam's Sons for believing in this story.

Thank you to my friends Bill Fowler, Rick Onkey, Mark Wittschen, Steve Shames, Judd Vowell, and David Little for being early readers and providing encouragement.

My brother, Bo Bailey, is my favorite golfing partner, and it was a round with Bo and Dad at East Lake that planted the first seed for this story.

My friend Rob Clark, the director of golf at The Ledges, set up our round at East Lake and played with us that day. Thank you to Rob for a priceless memory and for being a great friend to my family.

My father-in-law, Dr. Jim Davis, was an early reader and has been a constant source of positive energy and enthusiasm.

My sister-in-law, Denise Burroughs, a longtime AP English and Literature teacher for Cullman High School, read an early draft, and her critique was a tremendous help as well as a confidence builder.

My wonderful friends Joe and Foncie Bullard were both early readers and are two of the finest people I know.

Finally, this story would have never happened without the love, support, and influence of my father, Randy Bailey. I love and miss you, Dad.

A CONVERSATION WITH ROBERT BAILEY

It's interesting to learn that you are a bestselling author of multiple thriller novels. What inspired you to dive into a different genre and write *The Golfer's Carol*?

In April 2016, my dad, who loved the game of golf, was diagnosed with lung cancer. A few months later, my wife, Dixie, was also diagnosed with lung cancer. Dad died before realizing his dream of playing the four courses of his golfing heroes. *The Golfer's Carol* was my way of turning my dad's dream into a fable that might help people undergoing hard times. It was also therapy for me. In telling this story, I mourned my father, who we lost, but also celebrated my wife, who survived and is now cancer free.

There is such a wonderful appreciation and knowledge of golf, and sports in general, that is felt so vividly in these pages. What is your connection to golf, and do you have a favorite sport to either play or watch?

I played on the golf team at Huntsville High School and also played three years of golf on the team at Davidson College. Golf is my favorite sport to play and my second favorite to watch. My favorite sport to watch is football and, in particular, Alabama football. Roll Tide!

How did you come to Randy Clark's character? Is he inspired by a real person, or people?

Randy Clark's name was inspired by my father, Randy Bailey. I suspect the character was also inspired some by me, as I played college golf though I never had any aspirations of being a pro golfer. Outside of that, the character himself is pure fiction.

How did you come up with Randy's father's motto, "There comes a point in every man's life when he realizes that he's not going to be Joe Namath"? Do you believe in this saying? Why or why not?

This is something my own father told me when I was in college, but he did not use it the same context as Randy Clark's father. I think the point my dad was trying to make is that not everyone is a rock star. You have to figure out what you want and what you were meant to do, which I do believe. I twisted the meaning behind the saying a little to fit the purposes of my story and to create conflict between Randy and his father. I never questioned for a minute my dad's belief in me, as Randy does in this story.

What is one life lesson that you've carried with you throughout your life? Was it difficult crafting these four lessons in the novel? Were they imparted to you or did you come to them on your own through experience?

You have to believe in yourself and believe that you are going to achieve your goals. Belief is so important. Once I came to the idea behind *The Golfer's Carol*, which was to tell a story inspired by *A Christmas Carol* but with a golf backdrop, the evolution of the four characters involved and the lessons described were fairly natural and organic. The most important lesson in the novel was the last one. I think it's such an important lesson especially in the makeup of families.

If you could choose to play a round of golf with four of your heroes, who would they be, and why?

(1) Dad; (2) my brother, Bo; (3) Tiger Woods; and (4) Jack Nicklaus. I played so many rounds of golf with Dad and Bo over the years. Dad was my ultimate hero, but I've learned a lot from my younger brother as well. Tiger and Jack are the two greatest players of all time, and they have both been my favorite players at different points in my life.

***The Golfer's Carol* feels like a modern twist on classic themes of adversity, tragedy, and redemption. Do you have a favorite holiday or sports movie? If so, what is it and why?**

My story was inspired by *A Christmas Carol*, *It's a Wonderful Life*, and *Field of Dreams*. I love all three of these classics. I have always loved sports-themed inspirational movies. *The Natural* and *Hoosiers* are also favorites of mine.

What do you want readers to take away from *The Golfer's Carol*?

Hope. Hope that things will get better even in the darkest of times. Hope that they can mend relationships and hope in a better tomorrow.

Without giving anything away, did you always know how the story would end?

Yes. The final round and the emotions evoked when Randy's voyage of discovery comes to a close were always in my mind. Everything that comes before is a buildup to it. I felt that the real life ending of the 1986 Masters was a nice parallel to the vibe I was hoping to create with Randy's thoughts and feelings.

What's next for you?

My eighth thriller, *Rich Blood*, releases in September 2022 and the follow-up book will come out in 2023. I also have a few standalone projects I'm working on.

Robert Bailey is the *Wall Street Journal* bestselling author of *Rich Blood*, *The Wrong Side*, *Legacy of Lies* and the critically acclaimed McMurtrie and Drake Legal Thrillers series, which includes *The Professor*, *Between Black and White*, *The Last Trial*, and *The Final Reckoning*. An experienced trial lawyer for more than twenty years and an avid golfer who made All City as a senior in high school at Huntsville High and played three years of golf for Davidson College, he now lives in his hometown of Huntsville, Alabama, with his wife and three children.

VISIT ROBERT BAILEY ONLINE

RobertBaileyBooks.com
RobertBaileyBooks
RBaileyBooks